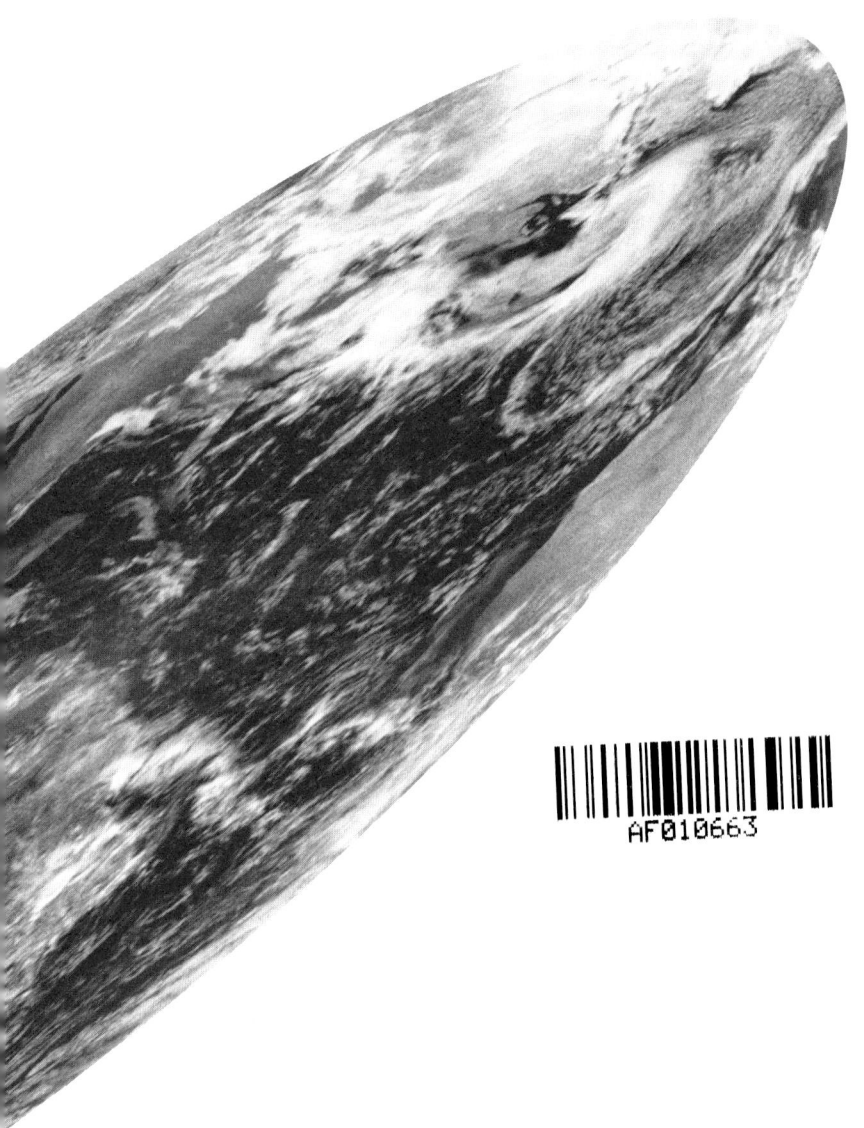

TOOLS FOR EXTINCTION

LOLLI

TABLE OF CONTENTS

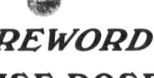

FOREWORD
DENISE ROSE HANSEN
7

SPRING REPORT FROM DENMARK
NAJA MARIE AIDT
11

ASHAN
VI KHI NAO
15

TRANSMISSION
JEAN-BAPTISTE DEL AMO
19

THE DISPOSSESSED
JOANNA WALSH
23

AFFINITY GROUP
ANNA ZETT
29

METAPHOR
OLIVIA SUDJIC
41

EMPTY STREETS
ENRIQUE VILA-MATAS
43

CADENA DE AMOR
MARA COSON
47

DRAFT
MICHAEL SALU
51

TUESDAY
PATRÍCIA PORTELA
59

A PENNY IS A PENNY IS A PENNY
JAKUTA ALIKAVAZOVIC
71

BOTTLE VERSUS BREAST
OLGA RAVN
75

LAST NIGHT I DREAMT I WAS MAKING A CONVINCING ARGUMENT FOR THE WORLD BEING A GOOD PLACE
INGER WOLD LUND
77

STILL LIFE WITH FLASHING TOOTHBRUSH
CHRISTINA HESSELHOLDT
85

KRAKK KRAKK
JON FOSSE
89

A FABLE
EMILIO FRAIA
99

AFTER A PERIOD OF RESENTMENT
LUCIE ELVEN
103

SIGNAL FLARE
FRODE GRYTTEN
105

BIOGRAPHIES
108

ACKNOWLEDGE-MENTS
116

FOREWORD
DENISE ROSE HANSEN

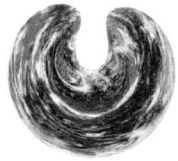

How to begin an introduction to the end of the world as we know it? Perhaps by questioning what we have come to know as 'normalcy' in the first place.

Museums, cinemas, theatres, libraries, schools, universities, restaurants and shops, along with many other public and private places that are both billions of people's workplaces and the cornerstones of our shared culture, have been forced to shut their doors. We find ourselves in the midst of an immeasurable crisis, of which the political, economic, social, psychological and environmental effects continue to be uncertain. There is no doubt about this. But the coronavirus pandemic is also lifting the fog from the fallacious Anthropocene idea of normalcy: that humans are somehow separate from and superior to the planet we inhabit. As a species we feel entitled to our normalcy, and hence will go great lengths to sustain rather than make-sustainable our routines. While the exact ramifications of the coronavirus remain opaque, it makes lucidly clear that separating natural, human and economic capital is impossible.

As Olga Tokarczuk wrote in her recent article in *The New Yorker*,[1] a new time is drawing close. When we're not working remotely or remotely working, we might be busy with (posting) our sourdough starters, reading the magnum opuses of world literature, and other demonstrative acts of slowness. But in fact what we are really doing, or should be doing, is 'readying ourselves for a battle over a new reality that we cannot yet imagine'. We can be sure that the world will look different in the future, just as has always been the case: this is the only understanding of 'normalcy' I am ready to defend. As it says on the back of my partner's t-shirt, which I have been seeing a lot of lately as the crisp work shirts have made their way to the back of the closet, we're 'Going nowhere fast.'

In *Frieze*,[2] Pablo Larios calls for the rebuttal of 'extrovert supremacy', a term he borrows from artist Hamja Ahsan. Influencers, forced small talk and social pressure to attend events and gatherings have no home in Ahsan's so-called pan-Shyistic society. His is an introvert society which moves against the continuance of the high-frequency sociability that is the norm, both before, but to some degree also during, the quarantine. On a similar note, Olga Tokarczuk declares having felt a sense of relief when the necessity of social distancing became apparent, instantly diminishing the disapproval that usually comes along with turning down social engagements – regardless of how many other invitations one is accepting.

Essential workers are risking their lives every day to keep society's foundation in place. For those of us who are working from home, and seem to have ample time for considering whether we are extroverts or introverts, the ongoing mass isolation poses an invitation to stop and think. Tokarczuk suggests that the enforced slowing-down might actually be a return to a more 'normal' pace of life;

that the hectic pace we kept up just 30 days ago was perhaps the wayward one.

It is in this moment of paradoxically certain uncertainty and contested normalcy that the present volume has been produced. The 18 pieces in *Tools for Extinction* take turns being alert to the old and ugly truths of inequality and racism: from the fact that all health emergencies affect the poorest and most vulnerable the hardest, to the idea that the virus is 'Chinese'. Common for most texts is a sense of enhanced attention to what is near, even when longing for what is far away: suddenly we know the names of rare birds and plants. With heightened awareness of mortality and earthliness, we turn to nature, to fruit and other forms of nourishment. And we look closely at our family, friends and neighbours: there they are smoking on their balconies, eyeing you in the bread aisle, or calling you, always requesting video.

With contributions from authors living in the United Kingdom, France, Germany, between Belgium and Portugal, the United States, Brazil, between Australia and the Philippines, Denmark, Norway, and Spain, this anthology as a whole is intended as a collective memento mori, with all the reflection and being-in-the-moment that might incite. A bit like items in the Voyager time capsule, each text is accompanied by its own anamorphic 'tool': things and beings we might suddenly perceive from new vantage points.

London, 20 April 2020

---

1 Olga Tokarczuk, 'A New World Through My Window'. *The New Yorker*, 8 April 2020.
2 Pablo Larios, 'Why Covid-19 Might Be Our Chance to Reimagine the Arts'. *Frieze*, 7 April 2020.

SPRING REPORT FROM DENMARK
NAJA MARIE AIDT
TR. DENISE NEWMAN

A morning in March, an evening
in April, the sharp light
sweeps winter away and birds
circle over the trees

homecoming, nest seeking

I think about my friends

    M in Mumbai
                N in Brooklyn
      L in London

a spring full of distance and angst
bathed in beauty, bathed in sickness

I think about V in New York
                M in New England
    H in Reykjavik
                  A in Florence
    M in Stockholm

SPRING REPORT FROM DENMARK

my parents, sick, lonely
cut off from our care

I think about D in San Francisco,
                        S in San Diego
L in Oslo
                            E in Madrid

my sister in Greenland
my cousin in Australia
my cousin in France

I fear for those who live packed in and poor
I fear for those who receive no help

haunted, nest seeking

For catastrophe I fear
in refugee camps, slums
for the world's poorest, I fear

for piles of corpses
hunger, fleeing
for the breakdown of all humane systems

I do not fear for myself
in a deserted Copenhagen

the sun so warm, the sky so blue

free medical help for everyone
the same rights for everyone

the inequality as visible as the tiny
virus is invisible

ASHAN
VI KHI NAO

Ashan wants to help everyone in the world because he has all the time in the world and he wants to make it a better place for someone or anyone. Yet, no one wants his help. At the grocery store, he tries to lift a basket for a young Asian woman and she stares at him as if he were a rapist. At the deli, he tries to remove the cart blocking pedestrian traffic so that two old men can get to the baguettes, but the men shout at him for trying to take their cart. Ashan doesn't understand why the world is so quick to misunderstand him. Outside, about to cross the street, he notices a small dog trying to eat some broken glasses and he walks over to shoo it away, but the fat owner berates him for being unkind to her canine and tells him very harshly not to talk to her dog that way. He droops his shoulders after crossing the street. He feels hurt all over and it is such a windy day. As always, the wind is so massive and invasive. When there are knives inside him, they leave slices of orifice in him, exposing his insides to air. His skin feels extremely sensitive. In the wind, there is nowhere to hide, especially in the open field. He couldn't even hide under the cypress trees because they are too tall and too skinny and there's not enough bulkiness to shelter him from the cruelty of the world. The world is a place where cruelty has all the swords. For each footstep he steps out into the world, a blade is plunged out and attacks him. At the bank, a blade hides between a fat patron and a skinny patron and out of nowhere that sharp object would assault him. With each attack he feels lonely and lonelier.

Some days, he stands in front of the kettle as it cools down and cries into it as the steam steams his face. Some days, the steam wears him like a mask and someday he would wear the steam as a mask. But this mask can't protect him from the coronavirus. What this mask is good at, is evaporation and condensation. This mask is a mask that should be worn when it's hibernally cold. A hibernal cold is a type of cold that can preserve its own visage and physiognomy. A type of cold that won't get uncold. Sometimes he weeps near the refrigerator and sometimes, if he is more sad than usual, he opens the freezer, digs his face into one of the freezer bins, and cries into it. His frozen tears are sometimes difficult to distinguish from the ice. He wishes there were a tear machine. It would cry for him on his behalf.

And, when others ask if he is capable of being sympathetic, Ashan would take out his ice-cubed tears from the freezer and drop them into a highball glass. He'd ask them if they could taste his sadness with their whiskey. They would nod their heads, but in fact, they are just nodding because his tears are too salty and make their tongues salivate too much to say anything. Once they finish swallowing, they realize that they don't have anything to say to him, so they just stare at his massive thumb and his tiny pinky. They study him hard, hoping that through their concentration they can make his thumb dumb and his pinky rosy as in salmon-pink, and that is the upper limit of their ability to understand the content of Ashan's hands.

He eventually walks home because no one wants his hugs or his help. He walks into the third floor of his apartment. He stops by the trash bin and asks it, Are you more sad than me? Or am I more sad than you? And, the trash bin is confused and refuses to answer. When Ashan enters his apartment, he sits down by the ottoman that looks like a dog and he tries to bark at the ottoman to see if it will leap over, hug and lick him. But, the ottoman is just a leg stretcher. It doesn't understand the language of affection or neediness. It doesn't know how to bark or sweep the floor with its ears and nostrils. All the ottoman can do is just sit and be a foot mat or a door mat if there is a door nearby.

When night falls, Ashan climbs into his bed and three large tears fall on each of his cheeks. He doesn't even wipe them away. He doesn't even walk towards his freezer to preserve them. He doesn't care if he is wasteful with his tears. He doesn't want to serve his guests his tears anymore in the form of ice cubes. He just wants to go back out in the world and help a prostitute with her job. Can I blow men for you? he asks. I am really good at it, he clarifies. But she shakes her head back and forth. She turns towards him, I don't want to be out of a job if they end up liking you. And, so he wanders the streets in the dark, hiding his body behind an alley, weeping to the dark, forlorn, semen-smeared brick walls.

What should I do with myself? Everywhere I go, I am unwanted. I am not a needy person. I have just been self-quarantined in a world that has been self-quarantined for three decades, since the dawn of the internet. People tell him left and right to social distance himself and to wear masks not made of steam or ice and to use hand sanitizers, but all of his life he has been doing just that. And, now with everything under quarantine, he feels invigorated with despair and desperation. Sometimes he just wants to run out into the street and kiss a stranger. He doesn't care if he gets the virus. He doesn't care if his lungs collapse. He doesn't care if he dies. He has been so socially starved for so long and that starvation is a type of loneliness that makes him feel homeless and out of place. By now there are a thousand knives of loneliness and desolation in him. He could not even pull out a blade if he had the skill or mentality for it.

At 3 am, startled by insomnia, he walks to the kitchen sink and pulls out a real knife from a knife block. Not an abstract knife anymore, but a real one. And, he cuts his wrist with it. The pain runs out of him and when he gazes into the eye that is made from the slit, where the blood seeps out, he realizes that the eye is a door into the thousands of knives that have been stabbing his soul. He realizes that he is opening the door to something he will not know how to close and it's from this inability to close it that he discovers that blood is a type of loneliness too. But, this loneliness has a name and that name is suffering.

TRANSMISSION
JEAN-BAPTISTE DEL AMO

My novel *Animalia* has often been presented as a book about animal rights, but I actually think it's more about the human condition. It's a novel about transmission: transmission of violence from one generation to another, from fathers to sons. It's also a book that investigates the relationship between humans and the other living beings we share the world with. The final section is about the collapse of the pig farm and ends with an epidemic that kills pigs, and threatens to infect humans and destroy the family. It also reveals the violence of a system built by men to generate more profits through the exploitation of animals.

A virus can be a revelation. Humanity has spent its history trying to escape from a natural order, defining itself in opposition with other forms of life in order to justify domination over them. Despite the warning and the scientific studies (about the climate, about animal sentience and the dangers of massive animal exploitation), we have decided to continue exploiting lands and forests and continue the mass slaughtering of our fellow beings (70 billion land animals worldwide each year and more than a thousand billion fish). To compare, the best estimations are that about only 107 billion people have ever lived on this planet since the beginning of humanity. Every year, we kill ten times more animals than humans have ever been on earth. We all know we are facing a mass species extinction. Since the 1970s, the population of non-human vertebrate animals has dropped by 58%. Fish may be gone from the oceans by 2050. Eating animals, and destroying their habitats, also leads to the possibility of new epidemics. We know Covid-19 originated in a Wuhan market where living wild animals are sold and killed for human consumption. Some would say, as I've read on social media, 'I don't eat bats or pangolins', and accuse Chinese culture. We should remember that swine flu (H1N1) came from pig farms and killed hundreds of thousands of people. Bird flus, such as H5N1 and H7N9, were transmitted by poultry. Bovine spongiform encephalopathy finds its origin in cattle fed with meat and bones.

A virus can be a revelation: it can reveal the limits of economic growth, of cynical profit seeking, of mechanisms of power in a capitalist system. We already see how our governments deal with the coronavirus epidemic, despising and sometimes sacrificing the more vulnerable of us: the elderly, the health workers, the cashiers or the homeless, to name but a few. Hopefully, this crisis will end. We will go back to crowded streets, bars, markets, bookshops and concerts... But we should not forget that this is an opportunity for all of us to be aware, to learn how to consider each other, to overturn all the systems of domination that we've built so far, and try to find another way to live on this earth as part of a community of sentient beings that we are not independent from, but interdependent upon.

TOOLS FOR EXTINCTION

On 20 March 2020, Fitzcarraldo Editions won the 2020 Republic of Consciousness Prize for Animalia *by Jean-Baptiste Del Amo, tr. Frank Wynne. Jean-Baptiste Del Amo wrote the above as part of his statement on winning a literary prize during a pandemic.*

THE DISPOSSESSED
JOANNA WALSH

My life in solitary is a lot like my life not in solitary which is my solitary life. My life now is more or less the same as it was, just I don't have to turn down invitations anymore. Now that my life in space takes place in this single space, my life gets more like this space, wearing to its shape through habitual movements. It is also a lot like my life in time, which is just an inch of time and things might happen tomorrow that make my life no longer like my life at all. The only reason I can say this is I'm not directly affected – yet. Do you think, if I were, that I could find words? Who knows? Words are only 'like' life or lifelike. I've spent my writing life, if writing can be called a life, writing about things I didn't have words for and I've found what I have to do is to render myself speechless at the start every time, or rather, work towards speechlessness.

**Instead of a novel called 'The Possessed',
I invented a movie called 'The Dispossessed'.**

To be dispossessed is, at its most basic level, to be deprived of the possession of life. And secondarily it is to be deprived of possession of narrative, which is how you came to have what you can call a life, which makes the life you have something separate from you; something that, if you possess, you have some chance to change. Being dispossessed is also a process and it takes place across time. Even when it refers to what happened to you in the past, you can still be, in the present, 'dispossessed'.

A 36-year-old woman dies of the virus at home in London. A visiting healthcare check considered her 'not a priority' for hospital treatment. Her husband fed her then went away to rest. When he returned, he said, 'she was already dead'. 'Already' is something enclosed within a narrative that is already over. The husband did not see the end of his wife's narrative that had finished by the time he arrived; he only knew it had already ended. It was story with no reader. He was not the reader and his wife was not its subject. Where was she? Somewhere else. She did not tell her story. Nevertheless a story arrived in which she was an inconvenient body that could hardly be accounted for, and which was swiftly removed by funeral directors in hazmat suits. Later, the story was read not by the husband, who also did not tell it, but by readers of newspapers. Sometimes the story in the headlines was that she was a 'Londoner', and sometimes that she was a 'Mum'. Very occasionally it is mentioned that she was black, and more often that her husband was a refuse collector, which is code to tell the reader they were likely poor. Who knows which of these was a factor in her dispossession? The problem, when you suspect yourself of being the victim of a story that is not your own, is, how can you ever be sure?

Narratives used to be about how you got where you are now. The future was open. From now on they work backwards from how you died, with death not an addendum but a defining factor. Every tale has a teller. Now only death will tell what sort of life you had, and it will define you at the point you were triaged for death, at the point you were deemed too old, too subject to an 'underlying condition', too insignificant, too not-a-subject to be 'a priority'.

Narratives belong to those left alive. But they're told about what has ended. That's the paradox. You can never peep in on your own obituary to read about your life and what it meant.

Image may contain:

In the meantime, from my solitary life, online
I see the strangeness of
    Strange men in domestic settings; shots of
    Men with sleeve tattoos in front of
ornamental mirrors;
    Men in baseball caps against floral wallpaper, men
    Unshaven, topless in shorts by knee-high
side-tables on which rest small figurines of ballet dancers with unnaturally
    elongated limbs and genuine tulle skirts;
    Men denied the outside, looking
    Only into the window offered by the screen
    As though they were looking out.

'Image may contain table and outdoor.'

This item is unavailable:

The more you move a story between your hands, the less shocking it becomes, the less resistant, the more pliable. This is the problem of first times. The first time you have a first time everything is fresh and terrifying. And memorable: the colour of paint on the doorsill, the crumpled can by the side of the road. You don't know where to go or how to speak or where to put yourself when you get there. It is not a story yet. When you come back a second time, it's no longer the first time and nothing is so fresh and memorable. But it's not just that. After a number of first times, even the experience of experiencing a first time – no longer, by the three hundred and thirty second time, a first – wears out.

The absence of stories equals the absence of contrails.
I am commissioned to write a story about
Things that used to exist.
And read it to ether.
I look at
Every celeb's name in
Twitter's sidebar and assume
It's cos they're dying.

To make a story can feel like being invited into a casino or, more likely, the private poker party of rich friends. You can do it once, but better not get addicted. It can be a very expensive hobby. It is not the hobby for you. You do not even possess what these people cannot afford to lose.

Pourquoi rêver a demain alors?

(Prada's ad in the March 2020 issue of *Paris Vogue*, which is, in the current situation, free to read online.)

It is licensed to us now to dream of very small things.

TOOLS FOR EXTINCTION

Lockdown is a place to dream from. This time I know I will escape. Or, if I do not, nor will the world. This time I am free to move in whatever world there is. Now I can travel anywhere, because nowhere exists except in memory. And every memory is a story: I've never been so happy. In my last lockdown (marriage, family) which lasted not for weeks or months but years, I was not free to move, in a world that moved without me. I could go nowhere. But I was very free to dream. And this is how I started to write.

I wake up in the city at 6 and hear the whole dawn chorus with no background noise.

The French writer Paul Preciado wrote in Artforum: "The first thing I did when I got out of bed after having been sick with the virus for a week that was as vast and strange as a new continent, was to ask myself this question: Under what conditions and in which way would life be worth living?"

A friend asks me for a response to 'the situation' for his magazine. I write back:

STOP PAYING FOR THINGS
STOP MAKING ART

AFFINITY GROUP
ANNA ZETT

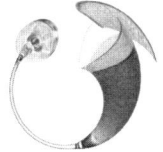

Just before Berlin entered lockdown, we were sitting in a bar around the corner from our house, lined up in front of the bartender. The bar had just opened at the end of the old year and didn't carry a name of its own, but Toma had started calling it Purple Bar because of the square purple lamp outside. So that's what it was called then. It was a one-man bar, dark, modernist, smoky, kind of expensive, with exquisite drinks. You had to get buzzed in by the bartender. The crowd was quite diverse, hard to pin down, various kinds of people came there, mostly German speaking. I remember a group of (mainly Afro-) Germans deeply engaged in a discussion on one of the first nights we went there. Another time we encountered a small group of people, white, not young anymore, with an attitude on the rougher end of the spectrum. When I asked them for a lighter, they confronted me with a question. Did I think a man needs to prepare himself for fatherhood? My response had been yes, sure, he should enter psychoanalysis, so that he understands how he himself was hurt and doesn't do the same to his child unconsciously. They were surprised by my answer, but very satisfied with it. (Psychoanalysis is not a luxury brand in

Germany, it's covered by public health insurance). The last guest we met there was a solitary bearded carpenter who lived on a boat nearby.

It wasn't that easy to decode who the bartender was intending to exclude by making it hard to enter the Purple Bar, except maybe tourists. Although he effectively excluded people without a home, money, papers, confidence, he might not have intended to do so. He said he didn't want tourists or any large groups of people to come, and we were only allowed to bring people we would feel comfortable leaving alone in our own house. One might say he wanted to run a bar where he had everything under control, but he would probably disagree and say that it's a matter of trust, not control. What was it exactly he needed to trust us with, his drinks, his quietness? Whenever I visited, the bar was fairly empty. A few times it was only us, a bunch of international queer feminists + friends or whatever, drinking beers at a table or personalized cocktails at the bar, entertaining this professionally dressed and flirtatiously dorky barman with our political and private conversations. The Purple Bar felt like the ideal movie set, the one where nobody was filming or posting anything on insta. We had each other to experience each other, until the moment was gone. Many nights of our pre-lockdown winter ended in this bar, and even though we were warned that the coronavirus would spread worldwide, we didn't talk about it until the outbreak struck Europe, and none of us had expected the kind of crisis that the coming spring would bring.

Two days before the city was locked down due to the pandemic and the Purple Bar, like all other bars, had to close temporarily, indefinitely, we got into a political argument with Hans, the bartender. It had started with a corona discussion, dramatized by the fact that one of us had just come back from Nordrhein-Westphalia where Covid-19 had started breaking out in Germany. Unfortunately, Andi made a joke about this in front of everybody. In response, the bartender and the boatbuilder, who was also sitting at the bar just around the corner from us, pretty drunk already, formed a spontaneous brotherhood of powerlessness, semi-seriously telling our friend that he needed to leave. They were joking, I guess, in the violent way that men from a majority group tend to joke when they feel insecure. In a second, the boy had turned into a carrier of the virus, a non-human danger, somebody to blame, mostly for the sake of it. A few times in the course of the night, Marc, the boy, needed protection from being marked and banned like this. He was too shy to actively defend himself, and at some point Andi apologized to him for having mentioned where he had just travelled from.

This half-serious attack on Marc laid the foundation for what developed into a serious ideological confrontation. Now that the pandemic issue was on the table, the boatbuilder said that coronavirus is just a flu, unaware that everybody had heard this comparison before, and that it had in fact already been debunked by scientists and journalists on various news channels for a week or two. We assumed the media could more or less be trusted, since there were so many of them and they had so far covered a variety of political opinions. But the bartender and the boatbuilder didn't seem to trust the media. Just a few moments later, the confrontation had already escalated to the point where Andi was laughing aggressively towards Hans, hurling at him the sentence: 'oh finally I get to meet one of those climate change deniers!' She was mock-excited about Hans's revelation, so as to soften her aggression, shielding it by some form of fake respect. During the course of the next hour or so, up until we left, Hans tried to move his standpoint closer to Andi's. He repeated some of her socialist and eco-materialist positions in a tone of voice meant to suggest these were his personal beliefs, but the damage was already done. He was struggling to hold the space. Suddenly it wasn't enough anymore to tend the bar and to watch educated women conversing with each other and speaking their minds. Now, suddenly, he himself needed to verbally make sense. Most probably he hadn't spent much time in his life reading books and actively discussing politics. According to Marc's assessment, Hans was from West Germany, born between 1975-'85, and had probably grown up with an apolitical, consumerist and hedonistic mind-set. If you're coming from a practice of consumption, rather than discourse, it's not that strange to blend various thoughts and opinions into one cocktail, shaken or stirred, getting your red thread entangled with various other threads. In any case, after a few minutes of discussion, there was no rational way out of this mess. General scepticism was mixed with nationalism, socialism, liberalism, materialism, altruism, unspecific frustration and the real-life worries of a bar owner. But there being no rational way out doesn't mean there's no way out at all. Until death, there is always a way. Since Hans was a bartender, his way out was a social one, and so he suggested that we become partners in crime.

If for Andi and Toma the exposed problem was a political and ideological one, for the bartender and the boatbuilder the heart of the problem wasn't ideological at all. It simply was to do with the presence of a boy who might carry the virus, dramatized by the situation that he was in female company and protected by them, which perhaps sparked some jealousy but also meant the problem could not be solved by kicking him out of the bar. Hans took a step back so that we could see him properly as he carefully handled the glass that was soon to be filled with absinth, gin, mezcal or some other fashionable liquor. He explained the following speculative situation to us: If our friend who had just travelled from Nordrhein-Westphalia today would get sick, get tested and contact-traced, this bar would inevitably get shut down. In effect, he would lose all his income, for weeks if not months, and all this would be our fault. Would we promise to protect him in this way, that when the police would ask us where we had been, we would not mention our visit to this bar? Would we do this for him? Marc and Andi laughed and I guess we silently agreed, mainly because we didn't consider Marc's speculative infection a serious risk.

It turned out that none of us were prophetic in our fears and defence mechanisms. None of us had foreseen that just two nights later, the police would be going round every single bar in the city and shut it down until further notice, no matter who had been there and who they had been in contact with. As we walked home and arrived in our communal kitchen after our last night at the Purple Bar, the conflict with Hans and his confusing political opinions were still on our minds. Toma hadn't been able to follow everything that was said because most of the conflict had taken place in German, a language she understood in part but didn't really speak. Even though she had intended to practice her German that night, it had been frustrating that she wasn't able to actively participate.

Upset, she recalled several situations where Hans had been saying things that now appeared downright nationalist or could be read that way, such as his outspoken preference for buying a German brand of tobacco. This latest political revelation made her both angry and disappointed. But at the same time she was reluctant to condemn him, since she very much appreciated him as a bartender. The conflict which had just taken place between bodies in space was still taking place inside of her, since she hadn't participated verbally. Andi, however, had already closed the case and didn't want to talk about Hans anymore. In her eyes, his opinions weren't to be taken seriously. His views had been all over the place, full of contradictions & repetitions of what other people just had said, and therefore didn't qualify as an actual worldview. Since Hans didn't even try to present a consistent standpoint or make an effort to argue for a specific position, his politics weren't even worth anyone's criticism. They were just a mash-up of various ideas that other people had mentioned in his presence. To me, this perspective made sense within the world of art and culture, where criticism was a form of paying attention and respect to somebody's position. But in this case I wondered: what if brushing off Hans's vocal opinions like this was just another form of denial? Perhaps Andi didn't care to take nationalism seriously, although it was a real threat with enormous social consequences, just like climate change and the coronavirus.

More than a month has now passed since Berlin went onto lockdown. In the meantime, Toma & Aïda once met Hans in the street, and he asked how we're doing for drinks. Toma responded we're fine, just about to make our own regular gin & tonics. Of course he didn't think this was going be good enough and he gave her his number, offering to give us a private home bar service whenever we needed. Edith wasn't there, but when she heard about it later, she thought this could be the perfect present for a lockdown birthday party at home, a surprise party for one of us. Everybody else would tune in via video from other neighbourhoods and parts of the world, safely stuck in their homes and sitting in front of their laptops. Those of us living together would be getting drunk in the kitchen on Hans's wonderful drinks, surrounded by flowers, lit by purple light, enacting the guilt-free, life-affirming Berlin dream of urban abundance to those in affinity with us. We would cry a little and laugh some more, someone would shine a light on the birthday child's cornrows, and all of a sudden one of us would catch fire in a candle and burn a large hole in their favourite shirt, and we would talk pandemic politics and dance for an hour across the Atlantic. Who is we?

We is not the same as I, and that's why it's unable to replace it. It's not better or larger than the I, it's just very different. We and I are happy together, at least that's what we aim to be. We are not in competition with each other. Right now we are neighbours, friends, lovers, but we could be any small or large group in space and time that isn't defined by identity. As a group we are not engaged in competition or battle with any I, or with any group that functions in an enlarged, collective ego-phantasy of sameness. Particular I's might desire to battle with each other or with other others, Andi or Toma do that sometimes, physically or verbally. Toma's fighting style is very verbal, focused on moral content & unbeatable arguments. Andi sometimes uses direct verbal offense, supplemented by indirect physical techniques like withdrawal of contact, which in this combination can be very painful for others. Edith prefers to be lovingly superior and if that fails, she raises her pitch. I am not so sure about Aïda's emotional strategies in situations of conflict, her voice is insistent, yet she knows how to hide in the centre of somebody's gaze. Marc doesn't pick fights. He prefers to be the one who doesn't yet know, the one who is in charge of the question. I think I am similar, so I get confused whenever I find myself loudly insisting on dogmatic positions. Normally I prefer to watch, listen and analyse. Some people tend to end up in battle mode whenever there's a problem. Surely that's because they were once punished by someone, or by a system, when they were small and powerless, and some part of them remained both angry and afraid. Some I's feel the need to keep fighting until they meet their final enemy, which I find annoying to watch, because it should be obvious to them that they will never meet this final enemy. Some years ago, Andi would have needed someone to tell her that she already met her final enemy and that she is battling blindly, in case she isn't aware of this, but I didn't describe it like that at the time, so I couldn't tell her. Outside of computer games, the final enemy is just the victim I used to be, projected into the future and onto another body. With the final enemy, it's just like with the apocalypse. If I refuse to let go of the past, I can easily predict what will happen if liberation fails or if love isn't found.

I have been wanting to write a lockdown diary after everyone was encouraged to do this by major newspapers, like they encouraged everyone to start running and to continue with their social, sexual and professional lives from home, online. Writing can be a refuge when an I needs to respond to isolation, loneliness, death. Text is the body I turn to when the person I need to turn to is dead, far away, or disinterested in me. But in fact, I have never felt less isolated than during this recent coronavirus pandemic. Right now, my social world consists of a lot of conscious touch and affinity, local groups and long-distance dialogues.

The world I had started working on before the lockdown, motivated by the wish to inhabit it at some point, was a world of relationships not rooted in identical I's. Identical I's are needed when it's time to battle as a group. They form a we that's there to make a weak I great again, or to make it great for the first time in history, forming an army of I's, a mega-ego. I know a lot of people who use this, as a crutch perhaps, helping them to learn how to speak confidently from their own body, which is rendered a minority, deviant, weak or dissident. Around here, I see Toma and Andi engaging in a political we sometimes, just like they tend to feel they're part of an army, of some kind of revolutionary movement.

In our kitchen, after the Purple Bar, before the lockdown, Toma said:

"In order to engage in political resistance people from authoritarian societies need to unite in solidarity, and which society isn't authoritarian, at least in relation to its most exploited or neglected members? Historically, democracy has never been able to exclude dictatorship from its theory or practice; dictatorship has always been part of it."

Andi: "If I had to fight for my voice to be heard, growing up as a woman, LGBTIQ, Black, Person of Colour, or religious minority, I wouldn't be the first to declare the end of collective identity, not until the revolution is over, at least. If I was expected to listen and follow, I need to join forces to make people listen to me for a change. It's about setting a boundary and refusing to discuss certain things."

Edith: "The funny thing is tho, when someone says: *I won't argue with you about this* it means in practice: *I will argue with you about this forever, because I will never listen to you.*"

Marc: "Hans, in the Purple Bar, didn't have anything to believe in like this and yet he acted aggressively."

Me: "Ideologically, what he said might not have made sense at all, but words are only one form of communication."

Whatever future we prepared ourselves for in the years leading up to this crisis is now taking effect. For us, here, it turned out to be the most meaningful practice to embrace the feeling that the I is never truly alone. It is always already part of a group and as far as my experience goes, a group is damaged when anyone gets hurt inside of it. In practice, an I that insists on being right will either end up sacrificing itself or it will sacrifice someone else in the group, and one way or the other its liberation will fail. But, in practice, the fact that the I is never alone is also what makes it insist on being right; it makes it seek justification. Even the mega-I of a group of organized fascists cannot bear to be isolated amongst themselves. In school, that was the hardest thing for me to understand. Why did the Nazis need to justify their violence legally, and in front of whom? Already being established as the total authority, having replaced God, who were they afraid of? Why did they need to make it legal to kill communists, after they had already killed them and were already controlling everything? They could install a racist, misogynist dictatorship and commit mass murder, all that in itself wasn't an ethical problem, but 'unjust' mass murder would have been unbearable even for them. The voice, or the I, of an other was still with them, they couldn't get rid of it. Even a white, male mega-ego preparing for war doesn't feel it is independent of the judgement of a larger group that includes more I's than theirs. Not even the most violent mega-ego is alone here. Even if I could kill everyone who is different from me, emotionally I would remain bound to the group I destroy.

This text has a we and it has an I at the same time. I went to a bar and talked to the bartender. I was with people. I experienced relationships. I fought and won and lost and didn't do anything, I worked a lot, said something stupid. I existed in language, perhaps mainly so, like walking on crutches. Underneath this text, in the underworld, I imagine a mega-I, an institution that has already caused a lot of damage. I must have felt something there. Other people must have felt things, too. It must have been horrific, or amazing, certainly overwhelming. Everyone had their own experience. Everyone is responsible for their own actions. Above this text there is a systemic crisis catalysed by an infectious disease and accompanied by a global order to practice physical distancing and self-isolation. In front of this text there is a group of people, it looks like the sun is shining, it sounds like birds are chirping, it smells like trees are having sex with each other via insects and it tastes like sweet water and the local bacteria of my mouth. We don't enjoy battle. We like to be happy. That's why we prefer not knowing exactly who we are. I am not just imagining us. We are a practice, an open rehearsal. No one knows who is part of it, but not because it's a secret. We are not a secret association, just a group that is open to change. We trust each other but we don't have a shared agenda. One by one, we are all annoying. Nobody is in the right. We can touch anyone and leave anyone's touch anytime. Currently, a physical affinity group cannot have too many members at once, otherwise this practice is illegal and will support the spread of the virus. Officially we need to live together or be each other's life partners in order to physically practice affinity with each other. The careful extension and conscious negotiation of these boundaries will be an important political task in the near future. We are essential, but we are not a business. Who are we?

METAPHOR
OLIVIA SUDJIC

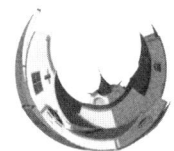

There is a ghost village in south Dorset
It was requisitioned by the government to be used
as a firing range
The residents gave up their homes, leaving notes
The situation was supposed to be temporary

The notice pinned to the church door reads:

Please treat the church and houses with care; we have given up our homes where many of us lived for generations to help win the war to keep men free. We shall return one day and thank you for treating the village kindly.

This is not a war. It is not even that war
My grandfather agrees it is not that war at all

Sometimes it is a breakup
Especially in the morning

I live opposite a silent school
It used to act as my alarm, hearing the arrival of kids
Their break times and home times, their absence on weekends

METAPHOR

These movements gave shape to my days

For the first few weeks I woke up too early
Jolted into full consciousness to read that the police have
dyed the water black

EMPTY STREETS
ENRIQUE VILA-MATAS
TR. MARGARET JULL COSTA

I heard a friend of mine on the radio saying that what's really shaken us up is the suddenness with which it came upon us – the 'thing' we'd seen on television and which seemed to us so very remote – the Chinese epidemic. This reminded me of an exhibition I saw in January at the Whitechapel Gallery in London. It was called *Empty House of the Stare* and was curated by British novelist Tom McCarthy. In that exhibition, McCarthy warned us that while our systems of control and mass-surveillance might seem rock-solid, they could collapse at any moment, because they are, inevitably, prey to glitches and malfunctions.

Indeed, McCarthy was saying that the problem of living under such a system lay precisely in those errors, which make the whole thing all the more alarming. One of the most troubling images in the gallery was that buffering symbol that sometimes appears on our computer screen, telling us that something isn't working, isn't connecting, a symbol that always provokes in us a feeling of terrible anxiety. I know that in some people's minds, the slow advance of the virus was preceded by an image not dis-similar to that ever-circling buffering symbol, warning us of some unspecified future disaster, but we could never have imagined it would bring about the collapse of the whole system, to the point where we had to stay in our houses and not go out in the street for days at a time. We never imagined it would come to this, but it has. And now, as we face the months ahead, all we can do is trust, somewhat naively, that, as always happens in extreme situations when everything is at stake, we will simply continue living and writing as if nothing had changed.

*

In Florence Delay's book of essays *La Séduction brève* (as yet untranslated into English or Spanish, and which includes chapters on Gertrude Stein and Giraudoux, as well as Gómez de la Serna and Pepe Bergamín), she writes that the pages that stay with us long after we've read them, the phrases and observations that surface uninvited in our minds like so many other memories, no longer belong exclusively to literature, but are as much a part of our being as our changing moods, and yet we always wonder why those same 'cards' keep turning up.

These recurrent pages, phrases and observations end up forming what Delay calls an 'insistent family' which, in some people, she says, acts like a kind of 'secret agent of their lives'. Fragments from our own writings will, of course, join that obsessive, comforting family, and this is precisely what has happened with something I wrote over twenty years ago in a book about Paris: a brief list of the things that for me constituted the fundamental reasons to despair. After all this time, I can feel that familiar list of reasons *not* to be cheerful coming back ever more insistently, a list, which, even after all this time, remains unchanged: the fickle nature of love; the frailty of the human body; the overwhelming pettiness of social life; the tragic solitude in which we all live; the breakdown of friendships; the monotony that is part and parcel of the habit of living.

The current pandemic certainly fits that second category – the frailty of the human body – but it also clearly connects with all the others, including the last one: the monotony that is part and parcel of the habit of living, although to be honest, living as we are at the moment with a heightened risk of dying, that feeling of monotony can seem rather ridiculous, because the situation at least has the virtue of reminding us that life is long, but that we fritter it away on all kinds of silly occupations (many 'self-isolating' writers, for example, have started keeping 'quarantine logbooks'). Why do we waste so much time? Because we live as if we were going to live for ever and don't, for a second, pause to remember that we all have to die, a reality that underlies the surprised tone in which people say they never thought to experience a tragedy like this, 'so far-reaching and affecting so many people'.

So many people? It affects all of humanity, and this is precisely what Rilke was writing about (in pages to which my own 'insistent family' returns again and again) in the memorable opening lines of *The Notebooks of Malte Laurids Brigge*: "This, then, is where people come to live. I'd have thought it more of a place in which to die. I have been out. I saw hospitals. I saw one man who tottered and then collapsed. People gathered around him, which spared me the rest..."

CADENA DE AMOR
MARA COSON

The bee is outside the glass trying to get in, the bee is inside the glass trying to get out. Above us the pink moon has just exhausted itself out of framed windows and into the morning and another day is lost in miscalculation. Sail away with me, to another world, and we rely on each other, ah ha, from one lover to another, ah ha... When you're gone, how can I even try to go on? When you're gone, though I try, how can I carry on?

The chain of love, the chain of fools, the bridge of love, the love triangle, the ornament of love and fools and string-alongs. Cadena de amor, that vicious vine that lusts for the worst of soils and releases sunward beaming blooms of pulsating pink hearts as it suffocates its hosts into night.

Who can now care what damned lover brought this vine here and in memory of what / who can point at the wall it first overwhelmed here / who carried this wreath over a sorrowful epitaph and left the vine to bleed across cemeteries?

Waiting for what he wants to say, waiting until midnight, waiting until all he said on television was this virus is like the vine, and goodnight and goodbye.

CADENA DE AMOR

And hold your breath. Hold it for ten seconds, and if you can't, then get some tea, and if you can't, then warm water, and then gargle, hurry and spread this message, gargle salt water three times a day, salt water will make the virus die, it will let it descend and disintegrate into the stomach... Neutralize, neutralize, neutralize... four pills of rhus tox in the evening, and after mild symptoms take belladonna... Dear all, what I am going to tell you is extremely important, ipecacuanha, alkali, plasma, be uplifted by hundreds of voices, I believe him, this man's been dealing with viruses since Windows '95...

And hold your breath. And get some tea. And wait for the sound of recorded bells at six in the evening calling out for prayer, as the rest of the time it's been birds. Do you remember, I said, that we were just slapping away stagnant water from all the puddles and pails around the house and we were just slapping away mosquitoes that ran circles around the heat of our ears. We were just clapping them dead before their black and white legs landed greedy on our limbs. I remember the body ache too. Do you remember, I said, that we were just looking out at the volcano, watching for the new shape of it, and if at the end the lake would still be within a lake, within a lake. It wasn't long ago that in this new year we saw other ends.

So quiet now you can only hear birds. But I am lying. Words of assurance. But really crash, raaaaaarrrr, the neighbour has made a chicken wire fence tunnel for her stray cats to move around – and stay there! – and it snakes like a vine around their house and all day you can hear thundering metal, cat hisses, cat sex. I said, OUT! Neighbour screaming at the cats. Constricting the house.

TOOLS FOR EXTINCTION

But really –

Words of assurance. What are the chances. Go party. We are in the tropics. It won't stand a chance under the heat. Thrash it out in the cockpits. We cannot be overwhelmed.

I said to the volcano don't you dare erupt! And it's been behaving.

Waiting for what he wants to say again, waiting until midnight, waiting… holding my breath.

I am sorry. If not already – Yo habré sido, tú habrás sido, él habrá sido, nosotros habremos sido, vosotros habréis sido, ellos habrán sido…

Many times a day I wake up in Stardew Valley. My energy bar is in full green and there are birds too and I shake apricots off a tree and my chickens send me hearts. I catch albacore and broken CDs from the docks and I sell mayonnaise. I go to the mines and kill bugs with my cutlass. But each ending day in real life before six in the evening my chest starts to tighten.

So when you're near me darling can't you hear me SOS!

And hold your breath. Ten… The sound of church bells tells me it's 6 pm. Did you feel that 4.4 magnitude earthquake? Nine… He holds up the blue pen and the black pen and one has to follow the other, there's no choice, and if you catch it, Eight… it's because you wanted it. The church bells meeting the sound of a tap meeting, Seven, the bottom of a pail. Meowwwww Six. Careful there are bees all over the cadena de amor. Careful there are thousands of pink jellyfish locking the shore. Five... Careful of the water. Dump the cabbages with cholera let the heads bob all over the port. Four... Smell the piss drying as the sun leaves the sky. Stay under the sun to kill the vee-rus. I said, OUT! Three. The mosquito is hovering around my ear again. Clap it dead. No blood inside. Two. Is that a cat crying or is it me?

And if any of the above occur, please take hot water with lemon and drink.

DRAFT
MICHAEL SALU

Every evening in the naked tree by my window
a pair of pigeons
huddle together on a branch.
As their necks retract for some privacy,
possibly even some priceless sleep I could envy,
I wonder
if they are as confused as I am
about a spring that didn't arrive.

Beyond the gnarled bones of this tree
the U-bahn still passes.
Ghostly.
Can't spot a passenger.
Barely any cars
but the frequent whine of sirens.

One
then two
then three
strokes from a furious wank,
then another
breath clouding up more windows
through which I gaze at friends

gazing back
with nothing.

Silent philosophies
loiter in front of green screen memories
of what we suddenly realised
had suddenly
become the sodden past.

Occasional words do escape,
their respective flight paths restricted,
filtered through echo
and clipped by tremors,
compression rates jolt pre-selected channels
on our grainy old boxes.

Conflicting,
like the lies told in order for you
to ride me blind into fear.
There are hooded crows in Berlin
I heard they enjoy feeding on dead animals.
One perches on a black Prius,
its head cocks.

We moved in parabola,
cautious around foreign objects like we are around grief.
I catch the calm voice of my mother
in sewn-on pockets of respite,
slim resistance
to the wayward currents
of stage-managed WhatsApp dramas.

Some big batteries,

TOOLS FOR EXTINCTION

small batteries, please
and the many practices of lemon preservation.
Some were suggested by an old school friend
and her air raid siren of a yell
mostly out of irritation but also possibly mild amusement
at my impudence and the stick I found
to annoyingly prod her back in english literature class
but only after the english teacher
had gone home.

Prior, she had spoken to us in hushed tones
attempting to relay the fragile gravity
of human existence
to our youthful insolence,
aiming to put us in thrall to the spectre
of the invisible
that could at some unexpected moment
become visible in the way
it bled out from a single axis,
to billowing across lines
through a billion coordinates
a hovering lantern of terror-beauty
staining the hem of our white dress
spreading itself nonchalantly out through
the sedimentary earth
and its red clay,
and its layers of bones,
and consolidated grievances.

Cormorants emerged from a dust storm
in Northern Africa.
They say the desert enriches the sea.
My brother came home without his mind

at precisely the wrong moment
but Mother just said 'come what may'
her freezer has been full.

There is repetition and there is routine
my own reality
emerges from prison.
5G imaginings immerse in the shit self,
I crafted a digital garden,
hurriedly sketched from a fading consciousness.

The hooded crow made a small jig
from one scrawny black foot to the other
inside my garden composed
almost entirely of downloaded three-dimensional models
of flora.

First I placed a young Aspen,
then a Crack Willow,
next to that a young Diffenbachia.
It was my imagination
replacing the physical one that got buried
under the weight of you or me not deemed **priority**.
'Yeah, yeah you dun know cuz!
It's that dark shit we always knew.
That dark
historically murderous
economically exploitative
passive aggressive
dark shit.
You dun know'.

I lack soap to remove the red dust

TOOLS FOR EXTINCTION

from the red earth
on my hands
it nurtures my garden,
it is reminiscent of home.

The other home,
coordinates slightly north of the equator
sprawling from a curved inlet
where necessity keep many outside
hustling on the red earth
within range of my digital garden
the love of my life had yet to atrophy.

I parsed my hand up against the glass to meet theirs,
they suggested expensive lingerie
'We can at least keep the dissonance interesting'
close your eyes they said,
imagine running your finger under the glittering elastic.
I did, falling flat against the soft.

The softness.

Whilst my neighbour silently smokes
on his small balcony
the same way he always has
but without the din down below to drown out
his,
or rather my,
existential anguish
about a lung blackened
hacked and vulnerable
to particles gusted along imperceptibly.

DRAFT

Though he (my neighbour),
mind,
seems little bothered
by any of the silence down below
his face as sullen as it had been last spring
his moustache a little greyer
his Maine Coon perched.

A regal, orange gift lazily eyeing the hushed shadows
the bare tarmac
the rattle of said ambulances.

I looked at the bright sun
from behind the glass of my kitchen window
and it felt like the earth
was chuckling in that sardonic way that it can.
Then it snowed.

There appears to be a permanence in things
but an impermanence in thinking.

So I will be alone in my decisions.
Alone in the decisions made on my behalf.
Alone in the thoughts I think I will have
and the opinions I think I will express.
A din over our decentralised strategising.
A white noise for breakfast.
The bits in my juice,
I didn't choose those.

Did we in servitude simply follow our masters?
Encasing our deaths in their tombs
encrusted with salt from our tears

TOOLS FOR EXTINCTION

falling in realtime upon the Phoenician's wares
that our masters insisted
must rest alongside their cosmic bones
as they journeyed on ahead
to the next ball of dust.

TUESDAY
PATRÍCIA PORTELA
TR. RAHUL BERY

I'm only writing this letter to hold it against my chest as if you'd written it to me instead of me to you.
– Maria José

I really need a holiday right now. I haven't left the country for seven years, haven't spent one weekend away from the house, it's always work, work work... I never have time for anything else...

Last year I almost went to Scotland. I was planning to go there to celebrate my 40th birthday. I wanted to do something to mark the occasion, and to go in search of my roots, of the Scottish great-grandfather I've never met.

I'd always dreamt of going to Scotland with Yves. We´d take the car, cross the channel, catch a ferry, then another, the two of us together, Yves also had a thing for Scotland, we both spoke English and it was all agreed, we'd arrive there on August 15th, my birthday, and we had it all planned out: maps, where to stay, an itinerary of all the places we were going to visit, the location of my great-grandfather's restaurant, all prepared a year in advance. But then in May, Yves broke up with me after 12 years together; he left the house, said he was confused,

TUESDAY

couldn't make his mind up, and that he had to leave. I haven't seen him since. I was in such a state that it no longer made sense to go to Scotland in August, to go in search of my roots; to turn 40 like that, all alone, with no one to accompany me... I know I should have gone but it would have been mad to go and spend a fortune all on my own, when there's never enough money as it is. It didn't seem like a good idea... to just go out there and do what exactly, without Yves? Guilherme tried to get me to go to Crete with him, we have some friends who've been living out there for a while now, and I've always dreamt of going to Crete, Crete, Greece, we'd go together, stay at João's place, Tó would join us later, we were all single or divorced, no kids, and I'd bring a tent and we'd camp on Olympus, I'd reread *Zorba*, or maybe the *Odyssey*, I'd drink only local wine and talk only about films, I'd start my life afresh on that holiday; we'd spend the day taking perfect photos and walking through labyrinths. But then Tó said he was against using budget airlines and I'd already managed to find some reasonably-priced last minute tickets with three stops on Aegeanair when Guilherme told me he refused to fly altogether because of CO_2 emissions. So we did some maths and found we had enough to split the cost if we drove there, but Tó gets car sick and couldn't take that much holiday, so he was going to fly, and with just the two of us in a car getting there alone would cost us three times the price of a round trip by air. Better to go to Scotland, I thought, but I had no one to go with, and since I had to finish some work I'd had hanging over me for more than a year, I ended up spending the holiday at home, working. I still thought about taking a couple of days off, if only to clean up the house before the end of the year, but you know how it is, it's always more complicated than you think, you take just three days off only then for it to be bad weather, and then you can't do any work in the garden, then you wake up late and suddenly realise you've lost another day, and then there's the frustration that builds up on Sunday night at the thought of not having taken as much advantage of the weekend as you should have, and to top it off, realizing too late that there's no food in the house and everything is closed and now there´s only pizza, but I can't only eat pizza for days on end, I promised to go on a diet, and I end up making spaghetti with an improvised sauce made from the few ingredients I had at home and drinking a whole bottle of beer to myself, watching a movie on TV which, halfway through, I realise I've already seen but I can't summon the energy to change the channel... But still, I really need a holiday. If I don't get some rest, I don't know if I'll make it to the end of the year in one piece.

This summer I almost went to Iceland. I had a unique opportunity; I fell in love with a man who was going there on holiday with his son the week after we met. I confess I almost gave in and bought a plane ticket on a whim, I even thought about taking a holiday right in the middle of the month, so without further ado I took the time off, I didn't even need to use my holidays that week, there were two bank holidays and the museum was closed for a long weekend, and I'd finished the annual report which is the thing that takes up most of my time and which causes me the most stress at the office, I could even take a holiday without asking anyone, I'm my own boss in my department, it was just a matter of filling out the form and stamping it myself, it was a calm time of year at the office, there were no exhibitions scheduled, the building was having

TUESDAY

works done on it, it would have been perfect, he even had a place for us to stay, and Iceland was the country of my dreams, I don't know anyone there or anything about the country but I've always wanted to go there, and yet it didn't seem right to make such a hasty decision, I've been working in that department for 15 years and I've never done anything without thinking long and hard about it, without really weighing it up in my mind first.

So I thought it over and concluded it was better not to go to Iceland, I shouldn't be so impulsive, and anyway I was just getting to know José, I couldn't meet his family so soon, couldn't spend a week with his son who as it happened seemed to take a shine to me straight away, and what if everything went wrong between us after that, what then? Just sabotage this new love without having the opportunity to get to know each other a little better, at our own pace, in our natural habitat? No, not likely, and anyway I'm sure we'll have another opportunity to go to Iceland together. José protested when I told him I'd decided to stay at home, told me he would love me to go with him, but his insistence filled me with even more doubt, maybe he already had such strong feelings for me that he felt he had to take me to Iceland, and I didn't want to be in that kind of relationship, we'd only known each other for a week and already we had to do everything together? Better to stay cool I thought, I'd just come out of a relationship a year earlier, him too; we needed to give each other space, which is hard enough here, let alone in Iceland... even though it's a tiny country with few inhabitants and the strangest landscapes, the strangest horses on the planet... Oh, I'm so tired. I'm really exhausted, I don't have the energy to keep living the life I lead. 7 years without a holiday, how did that happen?

I don't know, man, I think something has to change, maybe I should go on holiday alone, but it would have to be to somewhere far away, like really, really far, I don't know, somewhere down south, I could take a boat, a plane, a train, whatever, take the silk route maybe? Drop everything and leave, taking just one small suitcase and three books with me and go off to the other side of the world, somewhere I never thought I'd go...

I'd like to go to the Pacific, and take a long time getting there, embark on a sea voyage lasting many years, with many bouts of seasickness, the kind of trip I always dreamt of but never went on because Yves always got seasick, always felt dizzy and claustrophobic, yes that's it, I'm going to take the trip I never took and never even thought I wanted to take, take lots of risks, try lots of extreme sports, buy a one-way ticket on the boat with the most easterly destination possible and spend days and days and days at sea, drifting in the middle of the ocean, drifting in the wind, to the rhythm of the waves and tropical storms... That's it... I need a storm in my life, I can already picture myself inside it, and below me, underwater volcanoes, the epicentres of possible earthquakes, potential tsunamis... that's it... I need climate shock, people shock, sensory shock, culture shock... I need to be in a constant state of amazement, panicking about pirate attacks instead of panicking about giving PowerPoint presentations.

Ok, so I'll go up the entire east coast by boat, all the way to Shanghai, that would be great, go to Shanghai, 5000 miles from the Great Wall, a five-hour flight away from Victoria's Peak in Hong Kong, 500 miles on a cruise ship down the Yangtze River, between the river Huang and the river Chang, yes that's it, China! See the last pandas, caves full of stalactites and stalagmites, bamboo forests, the Terracotta Army, waterfalls... yeah, that's it... I could take the world's longest train journey, I read in a paper that if I get on a regional train from Lagos to Tunes at 17:05, and change there for the inter-city train to Lisboa-Oriente, I get to the capital at 21:26, then I take the Sud to France via Hendaye, which arrives in France at around 11 the next morning, then I get the TGV to Paris, and from Paris I go to Cologne, from Cologne to Warsaw, and from Warsaw to Moscow via Minsk; in Moscow I have to wait for 18 hours and 25 minutes, I read it on a website, which is enough time to visit the Kremlin before catching the famous Trans-Siberian railway, which takes 6 days to get to Beijing, and if I really want to, I can go all the way to Ho Chi Min, and if I do that I'll have travelled for a grand total of 334 hours by train, from Portugal to Vietnam.

But Shanghai, China, that's the grand plan... The thing is, though, to really go to China, to really enjoy the trip, I have to learn to speak Chinese. It makes no sense to go that far only to then be restricted to tourist traps where everyone speaks English or French and not have the opportunity to see the real China, I've already looked at a few online courses and if I commit to studying Mandarin twice a week for a year and a half, and do two additional intensive courses, one in December, one in the summer, in two years I'll be reading light novels and newspapers with relative ease and I'll be able to use everyday language. 'You won't be able to understand Tang poetry or read Mencius in the original,' the website says, but I think it's more than enough for me to be able to travel with some degree of freedom, and anyway I don't even like poetry. Even better would be to link the holiday with some work or research I can do in China for my museum, it's always good to have a local contact or a friend living out there, it makes the stay more vivid, colouring it with the small details of everyday life that a normal tourist, doing guided tours, unable to speak the language, has no access to. But if I want my trip to be truly worthwhile, to make a permanent mark on me, I'll need to choose in advance which specific region of China I want to visit so that I can choose whether to learn Mandarin or Cantonese, mostly because while you can learn Mandarin anywhere, Cantonese is not an official language, and so I'd need private lessons. Maybe I can contact the Macau Mission and they can set me up with someone, or maybe, who knows, I can get to China via Macau, that might even be a good idea, start the trip in a region that used to be Portuguese, with familiar architecture, *pasteis de nata* and *croquetas,* that way the arrival is less overwhelming, and I go from Portugal to the former British Empire and only after having practised a few words and expressions with real locals do I venture into the heart of China. Yep, this going to China thing is no joke, all I wanted was a holiday, it could be anywhere as far as I'm concerned, but if I start studying the language then I've got to go all the way because once you start, it's not just about the language, you really need to plan a trip of this kind in great detail so you don't go in the wrong season, for example if I want to learn Cantonese and go to Southern China, I have to take into account the monsoon season between October and March, and the winds that roar in over the Mongolian plateau, diminishing in strength as they move further south across Siberia, causing dry cold winters with variations in temperature of almost 40 degrees between North and South China, yes it's really important not to choose the wrong time to go to China, you could catch a bad cold, or worse, get an

TUESDAY

atypical pneumonia or bronchitis, which is much worse, and on top of all this, they tell me that the best time to go to China is in the autumn, but I can't really take holiday then, I've always got so much work at that time of year, it's the opening of the season, and in addition I read in an alternative travel magazine that special care should be taken regarding insect plagues, which are very common in China, and for this reason and many others you should start getting vaccinated some 4 to 6 weeks before the trip, at the very least get the rabies vaccine and some anti-malarials, which is the most important one but also causes the worst side effects, like drowsiness, headaches, vomiting, diarrhoea, and if I start taking all this medication a month and a half before I leave and then can't go to work as a result there'll be a problem because I won't be able to finish what I need to finish before going on holiday and there's no one to replace me at work when I go abroad and if I decide to get all the other vaccines so that I'm completely up to date and fully prepared, as I always like to be, then I still have to get the vaccines for cholera, diphtheria, tetanus, hepatitis A and B, and the Japanese one, and I still have to protect myself against encephalitis, polio, influenza, and bird flu, which isn't such a big thing, nobody talks about it anymore but that was where it all started, you should never believe what the media tells you, and I have to get protection against rubella, which I never had, against meningitis which has a vaccine now, against yellow fever and FMD, nobody cares about that last one but it's just as important, and according to my calculations I'll lose a week of work just from dealing with so many injections, firstly because you never can get all of the appointments in the same place, each one is in a different hospital or lab, and then even if you do manage to get two or three on the same day they'll always be at different times, each doctor has their own schedule and worst of all, I'm afraid of needles and also I tend to have allergic reactions to whatever medication I'm on, doesn't matter how I take it, which is why I always make sure I have a day or two to rest and to go to the pharmacy to buy the antibiotics I've been prescribed... oh and speaking of pharmacies I mustn't forget to get something for *herpes labialis*. And if that was all I'd still consider going to China this year, but then there's the matter of the visa, and I must have the option to decide at any point during my stay if I want to extend the trip for more than 90 days, and for that I need to have a long stay visa, and it's not always easy to get one for these countries, in which case I'll need to do what some friends of mine did, go to Thailand first and request a Chinese visa at the embassy in Bangkok. Then I spend five days on the island of Phuket drinking cocktails, taking diving lessons, something I've always dreamt of doing, sunbathing and reading about Marco Polo or what the Chinese think about what Slavoj Žižek thinks about China (a tiny book, but dense and difficult to read) and when I get the visa I go straight to the first travel agency I see and book a direct flight to Shanghai on Cathay Pacific, problem solved. And if I ever need to renew the visa I can always go back to Bangkok and then on to Phuket again for more reading on the beach and diving. But if only a visa was all I had to worry about, you don't go to China just like that, without knowing what you're up against, there's always the problem of actually adapting to the country, even if you've read quite a lot on the subject, even if you've sorted out all the necessary paperwork well in advance, you're still going to waste the first few days of your holiday just adapting to the local customs and food before actually embarking on your

TUESDAY

adventures. And the more I consider this the more I feel that the best thing to do is to go first to London, to Chinatown, just to see what it's like, just to have some prior experience of Chinese culture. I can go on a weekend, which is doubly advantageous, firstly because I won't have used up any of my holiday getting accustomed to China because I'll do it on the weekend, and secondly because flights to Thailand and China are cheaper from Britain, and I think it's very important to go first to Chinatown in London just to see what it's like, just to get a feel of what China will be like, I can eat Chinese food with chopsticks, buy green tea and incense, go to a herbalist, do a bit of acupuncture and a bit of tai chi and a bit of karate and, why not, attend a calligraphy workshop too... What a good plan, going to Chinatown, it even has a little water channel, I saw it in a photo, with a typical bridge over it...

Ok, my mind's made up, I'm going to China, I actually think this is the kind of trip that Yves would like, things could be better at the moment, life is tough and he'll never come with me but I won't be discouraged even if the flights to London are expensive, I can always go to the Chinese restaurant just around the corner at Martim Moniz, which I've been told is the best in Lisbon, so I actually can start practising straight away, like I'm already there; I will order all the house specialties: chop suey with squid, chicken with almonds, sweet and sour pork, fa-si fried fruit and at the end of the meal I'll drink a rose or a lizard liquor in one of those little shot glasses they give you where you can see a naked woman at the bottom when the glass is empty, maybe there'll also be a naked man, and I'll get a calendar with a magnet to put on the fridge with 12 different pictures of the Great Wall taken from different angles, one for each month of the year, and in the corner of the last page an image of the Buddha I can scratch away with a coin, and as I scratch it reveals a number which enters me into a prize draw, and the grand prize is a trip to China.

    And maybe I'll get lucky.

Hey, thanks for stopping to chat. It's great to let off some steam, it's been ages since I last did that. This time I'm really determined not to let another year go by without a holiday. But until then, and because I'm too tired right now and because it's too late to go to the restaurant at Martim Moniz or anywhere at all, and because I have to get up early tomorrow, I'll go to the Chinese takeaway on my street, order some chow mein and rent some Bruce Lee movies. You can't say I didn't think this through. I'm starting my preparations with no further delays.

A PENNY IS A PENNY IS A PENNY
JAKUTA ALIKAVAZOVIC
TR. DAMION SEARLS

'Current events' nowadays – is that just another way of saying 'anxiety'? The other day, I started sorting my small change, and I couldn't stop. We have a jar at the entrance to our apartment that we empty our pockets into. It's full of small change, with copper coins the vast majority. It took several years to fill this jar, and when it was full we were all surprised. But since then, we've kept tossing our coins in as though nothing was different, so the table it's sitting on – 'the Grandfather table' (not from my grandfather) – was quickly covered with change. One-cent, two-cent, five-cent coins. I don't really care about the mess – I've even been known to say, often enough, unblushing, that 'Life is messy!' Until anxiety shows its face.

Now the anxiety has grown to the point where I have no choice but to take that jar to the kitchen table, sit down, and start sorting. An acute obsessional attack, you might say. My fingers feel the metal, and gradually the anxiety recedes, thoughts start circulating in my head again. Copper is known for its pretty colour as well as its antibacterial properties, which makes it the ideal substance for coins as well as doorknobs. Some European countries

A PENNY IS A PENNY IS A PENNY

are getting rid of one- and two-cent coins: Finland, I think, and Italy. Red-orange coins might be on their way to oblivion.

As for anxiety, who knows where it comes from? If we need to find a source for it this time, it might be an acute lack of sleep combined with an acute lack of faith in the reforms currently underway in our country. Perhaps we can think of it as a question of something being taken out of circulation: the idea of solidarity.

This nameless anxiety. Tonight, sorting coins helps me. Obsession is always circular. I've come back to my starting point before long. I'm not expecting anything new to happen. With every one-cent coin I add to my stack, I curse once again these people who think only about money. How can anyone think only about money?! (Which is exactly what I'm doing just then, of course – with my jar, my insomnia, my ruminations – but I had lost my sense of humour just then too.) The demonstrations across the country; the various groups of blue-collar and white-collar workers throwing their literal and symbolic tools in protest; people resigning – all rising up against this morbid logic that rests on the idea that a penny is a penny. A penny is a penny is a penny, I say to myself, counting my coins. Nothing could be less true. A penny is everything but a penny – it's what you make of it. It's a sip of coffee, for example. Or a moment of rest.

At the British Museum in London, there's a small coin on display: a penny, minted in 1903, showing the head of Edward VII. A dozen years later, during the women's suffrage movement, someone carved across the royal profile in irregular letters: 'VOTES FOR WOMEN.' (The suffragette or suffragettes behind this defacement were apparently inspired by the anarchists.) This penny haunts the imagination – not just mine, also that of Tom Hockenhull, curator of the numismatics collection at the British Museum, who not only investigated the object historically but also tried a practical experiment, armed with a hammer and awl. Verdict: It's slow and thankless work to inscribe the struggle on the face of authority. Could anyone believe otherwise? And yet, after a very different kind of slowness, we can now, more than a century later, find this tutorial in iconoclasm on the internet (and not on the Dark Web – no, on the British Museum's official YouTube channel).

In a period of protests, upheavals, and revolutions, it's common enough to see seditious slogans in circulation, written on the traveling public spaces known as banknotes. We saw such things in the 2010s – in Tunisia, in Spain. In France as well. Money circulates. Ideas too. Sometimes even riding on capital's back, for a change. An ideal is an ideal is an ideal.

BOTTLE VERSUS BREAST
OLGA RAVN
TR. MARTIN AITKEN

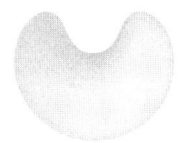

If I bottlefeed, the child is distinct to me, and I understand that he's alive. I'm filled with affection for him and feel bored.

In breastfeeding, time doesn't exist and I feel nothing for the child. We're one and the same organism, and I can't understand that he is something independent of me.

It's the bottle that makes him human. And with humanness comes devotion, restlessness. Evening.

Bottlefeeding is like gazing at an ocean, whereas in breastfeeding I dissolve into all the waters of the world. Without time, without love, without civilisation. In breastfeeding I'm under the surface, absorbed and displaced, fused into ageless nature.

As waves swell, so the milk swells through me, with the patience only nature holds.

This milk in me. In the child. This unhuman language of nourishment.

If the child falls asleep at the breast at night, he lies still and sleeps soundly without distress. But after a night bottle he kicks off the duvet and chatters brightly in sleep, like something under water that just now left its egg.

LAST NIGHT I DREAMT I WAS MAKING A CONVINCING ARGUMENT FOR THE WORLD BEING A GOOD PLACE
INGER WOLD LUND

This piece was first an audio work. You can listen to Lund's voice while reading by going to lollieditions.com/books/tools. The original audio work was based on printed matter that was supposed to be part of an exhibition at UNS, in Moabit, Berlin, opening Saturday 21 March 2020. The exhibition was postponed due to precautions taken to stop the spread of the coronavirus.

The audio work was recorded in the main bedroom of the small apartment Lund shares with her partner and his child on Fischerinsel, an almost forgotten part of the city centre of Berlin.

I am at home. I am sitting at a desk I have recently built in the main bedroom of our apartment to be able to work from here, as I no longer go to my studio. The desk has boxes and books as its legs, and a thin board of wood balancing on top for me to place my computer and my papers on. It is quiet. The kindergarten across from us, that my partner's child normally attends, is closed. The construction site that usually makes a low humming noise, even when the windows are closed, is also shut down for the time being. There are no planes flying over us. I can hear birds. I can hear the neighbours arguing in a language I do not speak. South East Asian? Mandarin? I can hear my partner playing strange tunes from the seventies on the stereo in the room next to mine. His child is playing quietly in his room.

At night, almost all the windows light up in the high-rises around us. Normally most of them are dark, as the inhabitants are out. I do not know where they go at night.

Now, everybody is at home.

*

You are at home.

*

Yesterday. At home.

I was tired. As I was lying on my sofa, resting, I watched a series of old movies about scientific phenomena on my phone. One clip showed how a volcano would react if one threw an amount of organic material equivalent to an average adult human being into the lava. The magnitude of the explosion was surprising.

*

Get up from where you are sitting.
Walk over to a window.

TOOLS FOR EXTINCTION

Look outside.

*

From where I am sitting, I can see a man leaning out of a window, smoking a cigarette. I have not seen him before. He is one floor above the woman who is often smoking cigarettes out of her window, always alone.

Before we met, my partner would look at her when he himself smoked cigarettes on the balcony. They never said hello. Never waved. Just stood there, smoking cigarettes.

Now, he does not smoke anymore.

*

A year ago. At a party.

A friend told me that she always wishes she was someone else.

I would choose you any day.

She said.

I looked around the room for someone I would want to be. On the balcony a woman was smoking three cigarettes at the same time. She held one in each hand and the last one in her mouth.

*

Touch your mouth with two fingers, the way you would if you were holding a cigarette between them. The way

LAST NIGHT I DREAMT...

you would if you were silencing someone. Touching their face.

*

Last summer. After an argument, a friend said that these days we spend more time stroking our fingers across screens than over each other's skin.

He paused.

Than over our own skin.

*

These days I only touch my partner and his child. Two days ago, on the playground, I told the child to stay away from the other children. Alone, the two of us built houses of wooden sticks in piles of gravel.

Today, the playground is closed.

*

Many years ago. In an amusement park.

While we ate ice cream, a boy was lifted from his wheelchair into the biggest roller coaster in the world. He was deafblind, and also unable to speak. Because his body was crooked, it was difficult to buckle him tightly into the seat. I asked how they could know that he would enjoy the roller coaster. They answered that all teenagers like roller coasters.

TOOLS FOR EXTINCTION

*

Wild boars are roaming the streets of Italian cities.

In Thailand monkeys are gathering at monuments where tourists used to swarm.

When I lean off the balcony I do not see much movement. I can see an e-scooter far away. I can see the canal still running through the city.

*

Recently, down by the water, a friend was holding his hands far apart. He was showing us the size of the fish that had started eating the birds when they dove down to catch their prey.

It's never happened before.

He said, and moved his hands even farther apart, repeating his words.

The fish are eating the birds.

*

Can you see any movements outside? On the street? In your neighbours' homes?

*

Some weeks ago. In an office building.

LAST NIGHT I DREAMT...

A friend told me that recently she had hung curtains in her windows so that nobody would be able to see her when she arrived in the morning. Wearing her formal trousers and a white shirt, and greeting her colleagues in the other offices as she walked by, she would then lie down on the floor of her office with her head on a pillow, close her eyes, and go to sleep.

*

Some nights ago I dreamt I was holding eggs in my hands. Their shells were so fragile that just being next to each other could make them crack.

*

Open your window and let the fresh air in. Just for a little while. Even if it is cold outside.

*

Some years ago. Early in the morning.

I had been out running. When I got home a caterpillar was making its way across the wall above the sofa. I carefully lifted it onto a map with an overview of different dialects in Sudan. Then I carried the caterpillar over to the window. It curled up into a little ball. I had to look at it the whole time so that it wouldn't roll off the paper as I moved. When I reached the window, I let the caterpillar down on the windowsill.

Afterwards I lay down on the floor to do sit-ups. While I was lying on the floor I was thinking about whether

TOOLS FOR EXTINCTION

I should have dropped the caterpillar towards the ground outside instead. I live on the second floor. It is unlikely that it would have survived the fall. Now it was stranded on a small metal plate. The odds that it would get anywhere else were small.

*

Close your window.

Notice how sounds from the outside almost disappear.

*

Walk over to your bed.

Lie down.

Find a comfortable position.

*

Two years ago. In my old home.

She told me she knew her ex was out of town. Still having a copy of the keys, she locked herself in, crawled beneath his sheets, into his bed, and slept. In the morning she made herself breakfast before leaving, cleaning the bowl she had used for muesli and the spoon she had taken from the drawer, placing them back where she had found them.

Some weeks later, returning from a journey, I moved the covers off my bed, ready to go to sleep, and found a pillow to be missing.

*

Are your sheets soft enough for you to feel comfortable? For you to feel safe?

*

Some days ago. At home.

I had fallen asleep without undressing. When I woke up, my shirt had left an imprint of a button on my arm. The mark was right by my wrist where the skin is soft. It looked like a third nipple. I touched the mark and felt a soft beat.

*

A few years ago. In an email.

She wrote me that after waking up, she had fallen right back asleep. Then she wrote that she had dreamt that everyone around her fell in love with her. She was like a virus moving among human beings.

I answered that I could not remember what I had dreamt.

STILL LIFE WITH FLASHING TOOTHBRUSH
CHRISTINA HESSELHOLDT
TR. PAUL RUSSELL GARRETT

'All in all, nothing much has changed for me,' he said to himself early one evening, because there was no one else to say it to, nor was there normally, 'people have been steering clear of me for ages.' He was heading up the stairs to his flat, holding his dry, heavy hands like they were hazardous waste, his possibly involuntarily virus infected hands, with which he felt a dreadful urge to grab the railing, the possibly infected railing, to help him up the stairs, pull himself up with the help of the railing. The lift had long since been cordoned off. The railing had always seemed irresistible to him: dark brown varnished wood that twisted with every turn of the stairs. The railing fit perfectly in his hand, smooth as a young leg or arm.

But if there was one good thing about all this, it was that his unfortunate habit of throwing himself (or rather shuffling, hunched over, dragging his feet) into the arms of practically anybody who seemed the least bit accommodating had been brought to a natural conclusion. He was going cold turkey and it served him right, because, to put it mildly, he wasn't exactly irresistible anymore, and who wanted to have their cheeks plastered with kisses from the likes of him? Only recently had he realised that people wriggled like eels to free themselves from his arms, even other old people. But he hadn't been able to control himself. Until now.

And who wants to do that, if you're going to die in the night, pass away in your sleep as simply as changing train carriages, leaving behind a couple of interdental toothbrushes (1 x light blue and 1 x red, both frayed and long since ready for the bin) on the bedside table, some grubby earplugs, the extra pair, and a half-empty mug of coffee topped with toothpaste spit, because yet again you had been so lazy or tired that you brushed your teeth in bed and spat in the coffee that you should not have been drinking that late at night. And in the middle of this still life the electric toothbrush, yellowed with limescale, toppled over on the grubby bedside table, sending its flashing red signal, ready to charge, into the darkness. Wouldn't that be a miserable memento mori to leave behind? And then the crowning glory: your body in a more or less advanced stage of decomposition, depending on when someone realised you were missing (or in his case, more like when the stench seeped into the stairwell) and discovered you. Your face perhaps frozen in an abominable grimace, as though changing train carriages had come at some cost after all. Your eyes, at least, mercifully covered by the sleep mask. And your ears deafened with ear plugs, which had begun to work their way out of your ears during the night and now looked like something quite insane, a wild contraption, a crazy idea, that gave death a positively comical look, yes, the ear plugs hanging halfway out the ears made the person in the bed look like a broken-down machine, and the cause of its malfunction was that the ear plugs weren't sitting right, so if they were just pushed back into place, the machine would start up again with a shaking, a rumbling, a sigh, a gentle 'oh no', so that everything could start over when the condemned's night was over.

So, he had started cleaning up after himself before he went to bed. He wiped off the bedside table and poured the coffee down the drain.

TOOLS FOR EXTINCTION

KRAKK KRAKK
JON FOSSE
TR. DAMION SEARLS

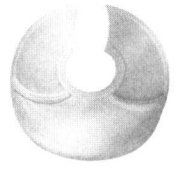

For Oddvar Torsheim

I live in a split-level house. The main room and the kitchen are upstairs, and downstairs I have it the way I imagine basements usually are, with gardening tools I never use, empty cardboard boxes, all kinds of stuff, but I've also put in a room and that's where I sleep, it's my bedroom.

And there I was, asleep like normal, when I suddenly woke up because there was a knock. I bolted upright, was someone at the door? No, someone was knocking on the window! I thought, should I get up? Should I hide under the covers? Why would someone be knocking on the window? Whoever it is won't keep it up for long, I thought, and I pulled the duvet up over my head and pressed it against my ears. I don't know how long I lay like that but after a while I pulled the duvet down from my ears and there was still a knocking at the window, but harder now, it was almost like pounding, bam, bam, or krakk krakk, more like. And now I was starting to get mad almost, because there I was, nice and sound asleep, and someone had to start pounding on my window! And it was the middle of the night, at least I thought it was. No, you know

KRAKK KRAKK

what, I thought, I'm going to give whoever it is a piece of my mind, I thought, and I jumped out of bed and stood there in just my underpants, because that's how I usually sleep, in my underpants. And they kept knocking and knocking. These weren't like normal knocks, I thought, it's like they're trying to break the glass almost, I thought. But now whoever it is is going to get what's coming to him, I thought and I marched over to the window and yanked the curtain aside and I looked into a pair of eyes staring in through the window. I stared right back into those eyes. And I took a step back, and then I saw two heads, and two pairs of eyes, and then I saw two torsos, and then I saw two fists, both of them knocking and knocking on the window. Bam bam. Krakk krakk. Two guys were out there pounding on my bedroom window with their fists. No, this is ridiculous, I thought. There are limits, I thought. They need to stop, I thought, and I grab the handle and turn it and shove the window open and I see the fists fly back and then they reach out again and grab the window and hold it open

Ha ha, one guy says

Ha ha, the other guy says

And I reach out between the frame and the open window and grab their wrists and squeeze them tight

Ow, ow, the one guy screams

Ow, ow, the other guy screams

And I think now they're in for it, imagine, standing there knocking, yes, hammering on my window like that, early in the morning, or in the middle of the night, whatever time it is, I think, and I ask them who they are, and they answer they're journalists

Journalists? I say

Yes, yes we're journalists, they say

TOOLS FOR EXTINCTION

What do you want? I say

and they don't answer. And I squeeze their wrists as hard as I can

Ow, ow, the first guy screams

Ow, ow, the second guy screams

Now we'll shoot him, the first guy says

Right, the second guy says

and that's not what I was expecting. They want to shoot me? What's happening? Why on earth would they want to shoot me? I think, and I'm not scared but I am surprised, that's for sure. Shoot me! That's crazy, I think. Someone needs to come save me, I think, and I look out the window and I see four angry eyes staring in at me and I see that behind the two guys, the two journalists, are two women. And I know them! It's Gerda and Gunda! Gerda! Gunda! I used to go out with them, first with Gerda, then later with Gunda. They were girlfriends of mine, until they didn't want to go out with me anymore, I think

Gunda! I shout

Gerda! I shout

but neither one answers. No, what is this! I think and I see that both Gerda and Gunda are smiling at me, so nicely and prettily, and they each raise a hand and wave at me

Why aren't you helping me! I shout

and then I see both Gerda and Gunda start laughing. They're laughing!

Now let's shoot him! one guy says

Yeah, we'll shoot him! the other guy says

and I think now I have to get away, I have to escape, I can't just stand here like this squeezing their wrists tight and waiting for them to shoot me, I think, and with Gerda and Gunda standing there too, watching and smiling, and they're laughing? Dammit, they're laughing! They're standing there laughing, both Gerda and Gunda! Do they really want me to get shot? I think. Do they really want me to get hurt like that, I think. Now I really need to get out of here, I think, I have to run as fast as I can, get away, I think and I let go and bring my hands back inside and both the guys' hands reach into my bedroom and I run to the door as fast as I can and I yank it open and I hear a loud bang and then I hear laughter, both women's and men's laughter, and now, what, what do I do? I think, what now? I think and I run up the stairs and I'm standing in the hall upstairs and I think the two guys are coming after me so I have to run outside, and maybe Gerda and Gunda are coming after me too, I think, because maybe Gerda's the girlfriend of one of those guys now and Gunda's the other guy's? I think, and maybe it's because their girlfriends each used to be my girlfriend that the guys want to kill me? I think, but now's not the time to think, now's the time to run, since the two guys are about to come running upstairs, with guns drawn, I think, and clearly they mean their threat seriously. Because that bang I heard, it was probably a gunshot, I think, so now I just need to get out of here, I think and I unlock the front door and go running outside in just my underpants and start running down the road on The Hill, but I can't run down to Town, not in just underpants, because there's The Co-Op Store and The Bakeshop and The Dairy and The Hotel and people might see me running by almost naked, or maybe not, because it is still the middle of the night? I think, or maybe it's morning? Because the time, no, I don't know what time it is since I take my watch off every night before I go to bed, I think and I run and run and I guess I have to keep running all the way down to Town, I think, where those two guys, and maybe Gerda and Gunda too, maybe them too for all I know, wouldn't dare shoot me? I think and I run and then I see a long row of sheep come walking up The Hill, one after the other, and the sheep are as big as cows, no, this, I think, I'm losing my mind, I think and I put my hands up to my eyes and I rub my eyes but I really am seeing what I'm seeing, sheep, as big as cows, walking single file up The Hill, but they're not looking at me and it doesn't seem like they want anything from me, I think, but there, down there on the side of the road, I see the two guys lying there and Gerda and Gunda are lying there next to them, one on each side, and the guys are aiming their guns at me, and now I'm scared to death, I'm done for, I think, and what now? I think, but luckily the house that belongs to my neighbor on The Hill is right there, so maybe he'll let me in and I'll be safe in there, I think and I run up the neighbor's driveway and I knock hard on the door

    Who's there? comes a shout from inside
    It's me, I answer
    What, don't you know what time it is, he says
    Yes, yes, you need to open up, I say
    Do you need help, he says
    Open the door! I shout
    Yes, all right, he says
    and I turn around and I see the two guys lying there and they're still aiming their guns at me, and next to them, one on either side, are Gerda and Gunda, and why won't the neighbor on The Hill open the door?
    Let me in! I say
    Open the door! I shout
    I'm trying as hard as I can, he says
    As hard as I can, he says
    and he sounds kind of angry, I think
    But the door's not opening, he says

KRAKK KRAKK

You can't open the door? I say
No it's stuck, he says
I don't understand anything, he says
Nothing, he says
And I grab the door handle and I shake the door, I shove and tug with all my might, pushing and pulling, but the door won't open
Don't break my door, he says
But you need to open it, I say
I'm trying as hard as I can, he says
and I turn around and I see two pairs of eyes staring at me and two pairs of hands and two guns and they're pointing straight at me and I need to hide somewhere, I think
I can't open the door, he says
and I see a rock sitting in the middle of The Field that belongs to my neighbor on The Hill, and the rock is as big as a house, I've never noticed it before, and I look at the steep mountainside that comes down to his field and that rock must have fallen down the mountain recently, I think, it must have happened tonight, I think and I think now's not the time to think, it's time to do something
I can't open the door, he says
and I don't answer and I dash towards the stone, it's as big as a house, I think and I run towards it and I throw myself down on the ground behind it and I think now those two guys can't shoot me, I think and I hold my hands in front of my eyes, but I'm so scared and so I get up and I turn around and I see an old man coming across The Field, holding a rifle
I'll help you, the old man shouts
Thank you, thank you, I say
and I see flowers sticking out of the barrel of the

rifle, a kind of flower I've never seen before, and my god there are flowers sticking out of the old man's eyes too, and out of his mouth too, no, this, this, I think, I don't believe it

Don't be scared, I'll help you, the old man says

Thank you, thank you, I say

There are two journalists trying to shoot me, I say

Yes, right, he says

and he says it like he already knows it, I think

They're lying over there aiming at me, they each have a gun, I say

Yes, I know, he says

Can you shoot them first? I say

Sure, he says

and I look around and now I'm lying in the middle of lots of flowers, the field is full of the same kind of flowers as the ones sticking out of the barrel of the old man's rifle, and out of his eyes, and out of his mouth, no, but, I think, this can't be real, I think, this is too crazy, I think and I think let's get it over with, if these guys want to shoot me let them shoot me, I think and I step away from the rock and out into The Field and now I see a dog as big as a horse standing there, completely calm, and it looks at me with big round eyes, and its eyes are made of fire, I see them burning and now the wind starts up, it's so strong that the dog is reeling from side to side, and I see that the old man, with the rifle with flowers sticking out the barrel and flowers sticking out of his mouth and his eyes has been knocked over and he's on the ground now and his rifle is pointing straight up at the sky and the flowers are waving from side to side in the wind and there, over there, there's an old storehouse on a raised foundation that also belongs to the neighbor on The Hill, and I see two guns pointing at me from around the corners of The Storehouse, and I think enough is enough, I'm going to sort things out with these two guys once and for all, now they'll see who they're dealing with, I think and I go over to The Storehouse, to the nearest corner that I saw a gun pointing out at me from, and, no, I don't get it, no one's there, no guy, no gun, and I go to the other corner that had a gun pointing at me too and there's nothing there either, no, this, I think, I don't understand anything, I think and I suddenly get the feeling that someone's looking at me and I turn around and I see Guro standing there so nice and pretty and she's looking at me, and she's smiling, she is gentle and kind, yes, she's really great, and she says it's nice to see me

Nice to see you too, I say

and I see that Guro is somehow full of color, maybe it's her clothes or else it's Guro herself who's every color, I can't tell, I think and then I tell Guro she has to help me, because I'm standing next to a storehouse, right? I say and she says she'll go and look

Thanks, I say

And then you need to see if there's a big rock on The Field, as big as a house, I say

And see if there's an old man lying there with a rifle pointing up at the sky, with flowers sticking out of the barrel, and out of his mouth, and his eyes, I say

I'll check, Guro says

and I see her pick up a leaf, and the leaf has rounded lobes, and it's bigger than she is, and then I see something white coming down over everything, and I look at this whiteness

Now that's enough, Hauge, a voice from the whiteness says

and I think how can this whiteness talk and also how

does it know my name is Hauge, that's my last name, because the voice from the whiteness just said now that's enough, Hauge, and I also hear another voice talking

Now that's enough, Hauge, the voice says

and I hear that it's my own voice talking now

That's enough, Hauge, the first voice says

and now I realize that it's the voice of Our Lord I'm hearing

That's enough, the voice of Our Lord says again

That's enough, my own voice then says

and I see two angels walking towards me, they're coming out of the whiteness, and they say that they'll help me, now and in future, they say and I say thank you and I lean into the whiteness and the pain is unbearable, I think, or actually I can't think, but now that's enough, I think and with an angel on either side I walk to the neighbor on The Hill's house and I don't see the rock as big as a house on The Field there or the old man with the rifle that has flowers sticking out of the barrel, and out of his mouth and eyes, and The Storehouse is gone, the two guys with the guns are gone, and Gerda and Gunda, and Guro, and the flock of sheep as big as cows, and the dog as big as a horse, and I ask the two angels where it all went, yes, the rock, the two guys, and Gerda and Gunda and Guro, the sheep as big as cows, the dog as big as a horse, Guro's giant leaf, and they say that none of what I've seen was really there and I'm walking in just my underpants between the two angels up the road on The Hill and no, no, now a car comes driving up and they'll see me walking around in my underpants, the scandal, I'm so ashamed, I think, shame, scandal, I think and the two angels say now they'll go home with me, take me back to my house, and then I should lie down for a long time and rest, I need to lie in my bed for as long as it takes to stop shaking, and the two angels will watch over me, they say and I thank them very much, and I think now that's enough, and the two white angels lay me down in my bed and spread the duvet over me and then I fall asleep lying there shaking and I think unggh unggh unggh

A FABLE
EMILIO FRAIA
TR. ZOË PERRY

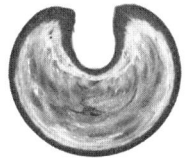

Today began the same as yesterday, which was the same as the whole week, another beautiful day. I work at night. It's a huge forest. I start at ten and clock out at six, but lately the hours have become less predictable. We're the only ones who don't stay home. Without you, they say, the wheels stop turning. The others recorded a thank you video with messages calling us warriors and heroes.

When I left the woods today it wasn't even six yet, but you could already see the sun was out. That's how it's been, sunny days, blue skies, crystal clear air. On the empty road, I am a tiger. Or rather, a fish, swimming between the plants of an empty aquarium. Once, before this whole mess, I was told I ought to have a child. Maybe when all this is over. But it's impossible to think about now. I lie down for a bit. I keep sleeping in chunks. A drowsiness that seems to never relent. When I woke, there was a passion fruit on a plate, cut in half. The seeds are held together by a kind of yellow plasma. They were pooled in one side of the rind. The inside of the passion fruit is white. It is a sedative, hypnotic fruit. My wife speaks to me, a voice from the past, I feign solicitude and warmth, but really I'm withdrawn, detached.

A FABLE

Before going back to bed, I walk around the house, check if everything is in order. I shut the door to keep out the draught, tighten the tap that was dripping. Some say the world's become more dangerous. I don't know. I think everything's gone back to being a bit the way it was before. In the forest, I take boxes from one place to another. I drive the forklift when needed. Have to keep the wheels turning, so they say. In the video, they repeat how very proud of us they are. But fingernails fall off, hair falls out, skin and corneas die, the body lives a week or two. I sit down on a park bench and my head slumps forward. Mouth open. I wake with a start, I look around, as if someone's caught me. I rub my eyes. The sun flickers through the trees. A liquid luminescence. I am alone in everything that is possible to know about the world. One day, I saw my wife walk out of a sweet shop with a man. They said goodbye with a kiss. Sadness is a soggy thing. Anger too. I followed him. I remember it had rained hours earlier, that's what I remember most, the cool, rainy cityscape. The man entered a cafe. Then he met up with a woman at a grimy shopping arcade, in front of a little doorway with a copy machine. They walked together to an office block. Across the street, I took a long drag on my cigarette. I decided to move. I went up to the front desk and asked the receptionist questions. I wanted to know where they had gone. It was only a moment ago, they just walked past. Lots of folks walk past here all the time, sir. I hadn't realized, but it was a hospital. Huddled, people waited for the lift, disappeared inside it. Others were released back out. Everything had a meaning, and without understanding, I nodded yes over and over. I tapped my foot. I closed my eyes. I waited for a long time, I'm sure I stayed wide awake. But they never appeared.

TOOLS FOR EXTINCTION

    In the kitchen, I find a cigarette butt on the floor. Life is a whisper, and we've learned to hold on to the items of the dead. A miniature wooden bear, with its front paws raised, in an attack position. Hanging necklaces. Blurry little thoughts: clothes in drawers, a lamp, vases, ants. Who will teach the dead death's demeanour? In the street, I am a tiger in a state of hypnosis. I fall asleep anywhere. I get distracted, nod off and spill coffee on my shirt. In the street, a woman pushes a pram. Every day it's sunny. It's impossible to know what day it is. In Morocco, the trees are diseased, the forest canopy is dry, their trunks sprouting. In India, the number infected is already over a million. In the forest, we work day and night. The country can't stop, they never tire of saying. You are the heroes who aren't afraid of death.

AFTER A PERIOD OF RESENTMENT
LUCIE ELVEN

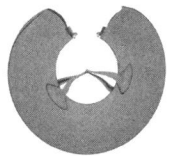

Normally in the office Ash is judgmental about other men's appearances, noting who looks horrifying and who is beautiful. Peggy asks colleagues pointedly why they are wearing their nice skirt today and suggests they try on her shoes in a way that they know she is angry with them and trying to compensate. They point at clothes: 'I think that one goes with that one.'

In the too-small tearoom, however, Peggy is drinking sparkling water and Ash is rolling his rs.

Peggy has a gentle, murmuring voice. She dictates and corrects him as they compose a memo for the wardrobe department: 'No – I detest dashes.' She pleads not to be abandoned when he goes away to buy her an expensive Earl Grey. When Ash returns, Peggy starts asking for his view, for his help. She repeats her questions. She leans on her elbow and readjusts the position of her hands, wrapping her shawl around her shoulders. She hisses when she breathes in, as though in a very difficult situation. She presses down hard on a piece of paper and pushes it across the table.

They have a delicate rapport. Ash tells Peggy about something another woman at the magazine said,

AFTER A PERIOD OF RESENTMENT

describing her as conservative. It is his story, but her expectations guide where he goes. Peggy laughs and inclines her head towards her companion. They imagine her, in the middle of the night, receiving a message acknowledging the arrival of the memo. When they joke, she hits the table with her palm. He gives her technological advice, how to delete the one mistyped letter instead of erasing the whole sentence.

They draft and redraft. She congratulates them both on their hard work. She has a clasp purse that lies on the table in front of her as she holds the Styrofoam cup of Earl Grey with both hands.

Outside on the streets, there are crowds, solid and real, a collection of pairs, trios, versions of groups that suddenly arise. They move into the sunlight, sneeze, lean back as if in a state of grief and confusion, laugh.

The tearoom is airless. Peggy giggles, holds her phone out to take a selfie of the two of them.

'Can I leave you to finish and go to the shop?' Peggy asks. 'Because when I go to the shop, I drag, and I'm scared you'll be annoyed if I drag.'

Then her murmuring is gone. Even so, Ash begins to talk.

He says that it is liberating not to be in that square study of his, pushing himself to make things up.

He has seen that Peggy is still standing nearby, holding the purse in both hands, letting go of it slightly and at once grasping it tight again, turning herself away from the table.

Peggy says she doesn't know what makes some rooms feel like squares and others like rooms. That's why she's recently inhabited a string of squares, though she harbours an old pride that she is very good at finding homes.

TOOLS FOR EXTINCTION

SIGNAL FLARE
FRODE GRYTTEN
TR. MARTIN AITKEN

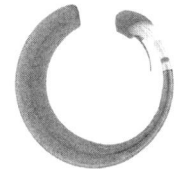

send word to
june, july, august
alert september
notify october

we're here inside
we're here in all our homes
trapped like insects
in the palm of a hand

we've cleaned the windows
for a better view of the street
we're connected to each other
by the flimsy civilisation of the internet

we confess to ourselves every night
but news rises bit by bit
from the basement and fills our
rooms with fear

advise the spring
clue summer in

SIGNAL FLARE

as soon as this is over
whenever it ends

find us, save us, deliver us
carry us out into the light

BIOGRAPHIES

NAJA MARIE AIDT was born in Greenland in 1963. Her first short story collection *Baboon* won the 2007 Danish Critics Prize for Literature and the 2008 Nordic Council Literature Prize. Her debut novel *Rock, Paper, Scissors* was published in 2012. In addition to fiction, she has published poetry collections, theatre and radio plays, lyrics and children books and been awarded many awards including the Beatrice Prize and a Danish Arts Foundation lifelong artistic performance grant. In 2017 she published *When Death Takes Something From You, Give it Back: Carl's Book* about the death of her son. It was longlisted for the National Book Award for Translated Literature 2019 (tr. Denise Newman) and shortlisted for the Kirkus Review Awards 2019 and has been translated into fourteen languages.

DENISE NEWMAN is a poet and translator based in San Francisco. She has published four collections of poetry, most recently, *Future People*. She is the translator of the short story collection, *Baboon*, by Naja Marie Aidt, which won the PEN Translation Prize, and Aidt's memoir, *When Death Takes Something From You, Give It Back: Carl's Book*, a finalist for the Kirkus Prize, and a semi-finalist for the National Book Award.

VI KHI NAO is the author of the poetry collections *Human Tetris* (11:11 Press, 2019) *Sleep Machine* (Black Sun Lit, 2018), *Umbilical Hospital* (Press 1913, 2017), and *The Old Philosopher* which won the Nightboat Prize for 2014. She has also published the novel, *Fish in Exile* (Coffee House Press, 2016) and her short story collection *A Brief Alphabet of Torture* won the 2016 FC2's Ronald Sukenick Innovative Fiction Prize. Her work includes poetry, fiction, film and cross-genre collaboration. She was the Fall 2019 fellow at the Black Mountain Institute.

JEAN-BAPTISTE DEL AMO (b. 1981) is one of France's most exciting and ambitious young writers. He is the author of *Pornographia*, *Le sel*, and *Une éducation libertine*, which won the Goncourt First Novel Prize. *Animalia*, his fourth novel, is his first to appear in English with Fitzcarraldo Editions, translated by Frank Wynne. He is the winner of the 2020 Republic of Consciousness Prize.

JOANNA WALSH is the author of seven books including the digital work, seed-story.com. Her latest book, *Break.up*, was published by Semiotext(e) and Tuskar Rock in 2018. She is also a visual artist, works as a critic, editor and teacher, and is an arts activist. The founder of #readwomen (2014-18), described by the New York Times as 'a rallying cry for equal treatment for women writers', she currently runs @noentry_arts, campaigning against ageism in the arts, and @zinesinthedark, a lockdown zine exchange. She is a UK Arts Foundation fellow, and a current PhD candidate in Creative and Critical Writing at the University of East Anglia.

ANNA ZETT is a Berlin-based artist, writer & filmmaker. Their often dialogical practice considers processes of sense-making through image, narrative, contact and movement, directing attention to physical situations that don't align with logocentric power and technology. With their work Zett has participated in various institutional and independent contexts within the international visual and performing arts. Zett is the (co-)author of two experimental radio plays produced by the German public radio. In 2019 they published the book *Artificial Gut Feeling* (Divided Publishing, Brussels/London) and presented two solo exhibitions (Zionskirche Berlin & Or Gallery, Vancouver).

OLIVIA SUDJIC is a writer living in London. She is the author of *Sympathy* (her 2017 debut novel), *Exposure* (an extended personal essay published in 2018), and a second novel, *Asylum Road*, forthcoming 2021. Her work has also appeared in a range of publications including *The New York Times*, *Paris Review*, *The Guardian* and *Financial Times*.

ENRIQUE VILA-MATAS was born in Barcelona in 1948. His extraordinary literary oeuvre includes *Bartleby & Co*, *Montano*, *Never Any End to Paris*, *Dublinesque*, *The Illogic of Kassel* and *Mac and his problem*, longlisted for the International Booker Man Prize 2020. He is the recipient to several international awards, including the Romulo Gallegos Award, the Prix Médicis, the Prix Jean Carrière, the Premio Gregor von Rezzori, the Formentor Award, the Prix Ulysse and the FIL de Literatura Prize. His works have been translated into 35 languages.

MARGARET JULL COSTA has been a literary translator for almost forty years and has translated works by novelists such as Eça de Queiroz, José Saramago and Javier Marías, as well as the poetry of Sophia de Mello Breyner Andresen, Ana Luísa Amaral and Fernando Pessoa. In 2013 she was invited to become a Fellow of the Royal Society of Literature, and in 2014 she was awarded an OBE for services to literature.

TOOLS FOR EXTINCTION

MARA COSON is a writer based in Manila. Her novel *Aliasing* (2018) was published by Book Works.

MICHAEL SALU is a writer, artist, critic and creative director, whose work and ideas find a place in a multidisciplinary practice. His writing, art and talks have recently centred on where the evolving semantics of technology, language and identity meet. His written work has appeared in literary journals, magazines and art publications including *Freeman's Journal* and *Catapult*. He is the former creative director of Granta Publications.

PATRÍCIA PORTELA is a writer and performance maker who lives between Belgium and Portugal. Considered one of the most innovative artists of her generation, she is the recipient of countless prizes, including the Prize Teatro na Década 1999 and the Gulbenkian Foundation Prize Madalena de Azeredo Perdigão 2004. She is the author of several novels, short stories and performances, including *Dias Úteis* and *Banquet*. She is a founding member of the cultural association Prado and is presently the director of the Viriato Theatre in Viseu. She has written chronicles for Jornal de Letras since 2017.

RAHUL BERY translates from Spanish and Portuguese and is based in Cardiff. His translation of David Trueba's *Rolling Fields* is forthcoming in June 2020, and his translations have appeared in *Granta*, *The White Review*, *TLS*, *Words Without Borders* and elsewhere. He was the British Library's translator in residence from 2018-2019.

BIOGRAPHIES

JAKUTA ALIKAVAZOVIC is a French writer of Bosnian and Montenegrin origins. She was born in Paris, where she studied at the Ecole Normale Superieure and where she now lives. She has lived in the UK and in Italy, where she was a resident at the Villa Medicis in Rome in 2013-2014. Her first novel, *Corps Volatils* (2008) won the Goncourt Prize for Best First Novel and her second and third novels, *Le Londres-Luxor* (2010) and *La Blonde et Le Bunker* (2012) won prizes in France and Italy. She is published by Editions de l'Olivier in France. Her new novel, *Night as it Falls* (*L'Avancee de la Nuit*), will be published by Faber in 2021. She is also the translator of Anna Burns and Ben Lerner and teaches at La Sorbonne Nouvelle.

DAMION SEARLS has translated more than forty books, most recently Jon Fosse's *The Other Name: Septology I-II*, André Gide's *Marshlands*, and Rilke's *Letters to a Young Poet*.

OLGA RAVN (b. 1986) is a Danish novelist and poet. Her novel *Celestine* appeared to critical acclaim in 2015. She is also a literary critic and has written for Politiken and several other Danish publications. Alongside Johanne Lykke Holm, she runs the feminist performance group and writing school *Hekseskolen*. Her novel *The Employees* will be published by Lolli Editions in October 2020, translated by Martin Aitken. The winner of a Fondation Jan Michalski award, it is Ravn's first book to appear in English.

MARTIN AITKEN is the translator of numerous novels from Danish and Norwegian, including works by Karl Ove Knausgaard, Peter Høeg and Ida Jessen. He was a finalist at the U.S. National Book Awards 2018 and received the PEN America Translation Prize 2019 for his translation of

Hanne Ørstavik's *Love*. His translation of Olga Ravn's *The Employees* is forthcoming (Lolli Editions, 2020).

INGER WOLD LUND is a writer and artist based in Berlin. Lund was educated at the Oslo National Academy of the Arts; Konstfack University College of Arts, Crafts and Design, Stockholm; and Staatliche Hochschule für Bildende Künste, Frankfurt am Main. She is the writer of two books in her native Norwegian published by Cappelen Damm and Flamme Forlag. A collection of her stories in English has been published by Ugly Duckling Presse. Recent exhibitions include Leviathan at Kunsthal Aarhus; The 6th Moscow International Biennale for Young Art; The 9th Norwegian Sculpture Biannual, Oslo; Wildlife Sculpture Park, Oslo and M.I/mi1glissé, Berlin.

CHRISTINA HESSELHOLDT (b. 1962) studied at the Danish Academy of Creative Writing in Copenhagen. Her first novel, *The Kitchen, the Tomb & the Landscape* (*Køkkenet, Gravkammeret & Landskabet*) was published in 1991. She has written fifteen books of prose, and received critical acclaim and awards for her books, including the Beatrice Prize in 2007 and the Critics' Prize in 2010. She was included in Dalkey Archive's *Best European Fiction 2013. C ompanions (Selskabet)* was her first book to appear in English. *Vivian*, her novel about the photographer Vivian Maier, won the Danish Radio Best Novel Award 2017 and has been shortlisted for the Nordic Council Literature Prize in 2017. Her most recent novel, *Virginia is for Lovers*, was published in 2019. She is translated in ten languages and published in English by Fitzcarraldo Editions (tr. Paul Russell Garrett).

BIOGRAPHIES

PAUL RUSSELL GARRETT translates from Danish and Norwegian, with drama holding a particular interest for him. He has translated a dozen plays and has a further ten published translations to his name, including Lars Mytting's *The Sixteen Trees of the Somme*, longlisted for the International Dublin Literary Award. Previous translations of Christina Hesselholdt include *Companions* and *Vivian*.

JON FOSSE was born in 1959 on the west coast of Norway and is the recipient of countless prestigious prizes, both in his native Norway and abroad. Since his 1983 fiction debut, *Raudt, svart* [*Red, Black*], Fosse has written prose, poetry, essays, short stories, children's books, and over forty plays, with more than a thousand productions performed and translations into fifty languages. *The Other Name* is the first volume in *Septology*, his latest prose work, will be published in three volumes by Fitzcarraldo Editions.

EMILIO FRAIA was born in São Paulo, Brazil, in 1982. He is the author of *Sebastopol* (*Sevastopol*, Alfaguara, 2018); *Campo em branco* (*Blank Field*, Companhia das Letras, 2013) and *O verão do Chibo* (*The summer of Chibo*, Alfaguara, 2008). A part of his second novel, 'Sevastopol', was published in *The New Yorker* in December 2019 and the full novel will be published by New Directions in the US in 2021. The book also will be adapted for the big screen. He was one of Granta's twenty Best Brazilian Young Writers in 2012. Fraia is currently an editor of contemporary fiction at Companhia das Letras, a publishing house in São Paulo, where he lives.

ZOË PERRY's translations of contemporary Portuguese-language fiction and non-fiction have appeared in *The New Yorker*, *Granta*, *Words Without Borders*, *Mānoa*, and the *Washington Square Review*. In 2015 she was translator-in-residence at the FLIP international literary festival in Paraty, Brazil, and she was awarded a PEN/Heim grant for her translation of Veronica Stigger's novel Opisanie świata. Zoë was selected for a residency at the Banff International Translation Centre for her translation of Emilio Fraia's *Sevastopol*, forthcoming from New Directions.

LUCIE ELVEN has written for *Granta*, *NOON* and *London Review of Books*. Her first novel will be published by Soft Skull in 2021.

FRODE GRYTTEN (b. 1960) made his debut in 1984 with the poetry collection *Start*. Since then he has written novels, short stories, poems and children's books, and his work has been translated into 15 languages. *Songs of the Beehive* (1999) won Norway's national book award, the Brage, and was shortlisted for the Nordic Council Literary Prize. *Floating Bear* (2005) won the Riverton Prize and *Rooms by the Ocean, Rooms by the Sea* (2007) won the New Norwegian Literary Prize and the Melsom Prize. A new collection of short stories, *Garage Land*, will appear in Norwegian autumn 2020.

ACKNOWLEDGEMENTS

Lolli Editions would first and foremost like to thank all the authors and literary translators who have made this book possible. It was produced at great pace in a time when circumstances were adverse and changing daily. Several people involved in the project even fell ill due to the coronavirus. Had it not been for everyone's enthusiasm and tenacity, there would have been no book, or it would not have carried the sense of urgency that is so vividly felt across the texts in the present volume. With a few exceptions, all work in this volume was written during the pandemic. For the sake of balance, and because certain pieces lent themselves well to the collection as a whole, pre-existing writing has been selected. Common for all texts is that they have not previously appeared in English. We would also like to extend a special thank you to the many literary agents involved, particularly Laurence Laluyaux and Gina Winje whose support has been integral and decisive. We are further grateful to NORLA, Guillaume Chuard, Daniel Kang Yoon Nørregaard and Daniel Royle, James Tookey and the Republic of Consciousness Prize for Small Presses.

The texts are published by agreement with the authors and Aitken Alexander Associates, Gyldendal Group Agency, MB Agencia Literaria, Oslo Literary Agency, RCW Literary Agency, United Agents, Winje Agency, and the Republic of Consciousness Prize for Small Presses, respectively.

The citation on p. 45 in 'Empty Streets' is from *The Notebooks of Malte Laurids Brigge* by Rainer Marie Rilke, translated and edited by Michael Hulse. London: Penguin Classics, 2009, p. 3.

TOOLS FOR EXTINCTION

Tools for Extinction
© Lolli Editions, London 2020
1st edition, 1st impression

'Foreword'
© Denise Rose Hansen, 2020

'Spring Report from Denmark'
['Forårsrapport fra Danmark']
© Naja Marie Aidt, 2020
Translation © Denise Newman, 2020

'Ashan'
© Vi Khi Nao, 2020

'Transmission'
© Jean-Baptiste Del Amo, 2020
Originally published on Republic
of Consciousness' website on 31 March
2020 as 'Jean-Baptiste Del Amo
on winning the Republic
of Consciousness Prize 2020'

'The Dispossessed'
© Joanna Walsh, 2020

'Affinity Group'
© Anna Zett, 2020

'Metaphor'
© Olivia Sudjic, 2020

'Empty Streets' ['Calles vacías']
© Enrique Vila-Matas, 2020
Translation © Margaret Jull Costa, 2020

'Cadena de Amor'
© Mara Coson, 2020

'Draft'
© Michael Salu, 2020

'Tuesday'
© Patrícia Portela, 2020
From *Dias Úteis*, first published
in Portuguese by Editorial Caminho/
leya, 2017 and Dublinense, 2019
Translation © Rahul Bery, 2020

'A Penny Is a Penny Is a Penny'
['Un sou est un sou est un sou']
© Jakuta Alikavazovic, 2020
First published in French in *Libération*,
14 February 2020
Translation © Damion Searls, 2020

'Bottle Versus Breast'
['Flaske versus bryst']
© Olga Ravn, 2020
The text is an extract from *Mit Arbejde*,
Gyldendal 2020 (forthcoming)
Translation © Martin Aitken, 2020

'Last Night I Dreamt I Was
Making a Convincing Argument
for the World Being a Good Place'
© Inger Wold Lund, 2020

'Still Life with Flashing Toothbrush'
['Stilleben med blinkende tandbørste']
© Christina Hesselholdt, 2020
Translation © Paul Russell Garrett, 2020

'Krakk Krakk' ['Kakk kakk']
© Jon Fosse, 2020
Translation © Damion Searls, 2020

'A Fable' ['Uma fábula']
© Emilio Fraia, 2020
Translation © Zoë Perry, 2020

'After a Period of Resentment'
© Lucie Elven

'Signal Flare' ['Naudbluss']
© Frode Grytten
First published in Norwegian
in *Vårt Land*
Translation © Martin Aitken, 2020

COLOPHON

Edited and compiled by Denise Rose Hansen
Proofread by Susie Butler
Graphic design by Ard – Chuard & Nørregaard
with Daniel Royle
Typeset in Media77 and Windsor
Printed and bound by KOPA, Lithuania, 2020

The translation of Jon Fosse's 'Krakk Krakk' ['Kakk kakk'] was made possible through the generous support of NORLA.

The right of each individual writer to be identified as the author of their respective works has been asserted in accordance with Section 77 of the Copyright, Designs and Patents Act 1988.

A CIP catalogue record for this book is available from the British Library.

All images used are in the public domain, CC0 1.0 Universal. Every attempt has been made to be respectful of all copyright.

ISBN 978-1-9999928-2-8

Lolli Editions
132 Defoe House, Barbican
EC2Y 8ND London
www.lollieditions.com